**"Is this your usual practice—
disable men and then
take advantage of them?"**

Pamela's gaze flew up to meet his, and she saw the mocking gleam in his gray eyes. "There wouldn't be much point to it, would there?" she retorted. "I like my men able-bodied . . . and able."

He'd been as stoic as an Indian while she'd tended his leg, but now he was making a major production out of a mere sprained wrist.

"What's your name, by the way?" she asked as she wrapped the makeshift sling around his arm.

"Yes, you'll need it for the insurance forms," he told her nastily. Pamela leaned closer to him to tie a knot around his neck and grinned.

The grin seemed to infuriate him, and he grabbed her around the waist. She suddenly no longer felt cold.

"Kind of cocky, aren't you, for someone who's just run down an innocent pedestrian," he said gruffly.

"You're no innocent anything," Pamela said, still grinning.

Other Second Chance at Love books by
Diana Mars

SWEET SURRENDER #95
SWEET ABANDON #122
SWEET TRESPASS #182
SWEET SPLENDOR #214
SWEET DECEPTION #234

Diana Mars *was trained as an anthropologist and has held management positions in the communications and import-export industries. Fluent in Spanish and German, she has also been a translator and interpreter. Diana's interests include computers, philately, tennis, jewelry, and nature tours. At various times, Diana has lived in South America, Europe, and the Far East. She currently resides in the Midwest.*

Dear Reader:

The lazy days of summer are here, a perfect time to enjoy July's SECOND CHANCE AT LOVE romances.

In *Master Touch* (#274) Jasmine Craig reintroduces Hollywood idol Damion Tanner, who you'll remember as Lynn Frampton's boss in *Dear Adam* (#243). Damion *looks* like a typical devastating womanizer, but inside he's a man of intriguing depth, complexity, and contradictory impulses. He dislikes Alessandra Hawkins on sight, but can't resist pursuing her. Alessandra is thoroughly disdainful of Damion, and equally smitten. You'll love reading how these two marvelously antagonistic characters walk backward into love — resisting all the way!

In *Night of a Thousand Stars* (#275) Petra Diamond takes you where no couple has gone before — to sex in space! Astronaut Jennie Jacobs and ace pilot Dean Bradshaw have *all* the "right stuff" for such an experiment, but they've had little time to explore their more tender feelings. Suddenly their emotions catch up with them, making their coming together a bristly, challenging proposition. Petra Diamond handles their love story with sensitive realism, making *Night of a Thousand Stars* out of this world.

Laine Allen, an exciting newcomer, turns romance stereotypes on their heads in *Undercover Kisses* (#276). Every time private eye Katrina Langley asks herself, "How wrong could a woman be about a man," ultra-manly Moss Adams suggests the answer: "Very wrong!" Every time Kat thinks they're evenly matched, Moss cheerfully knocks her off balance. Moss's intelligent deviltry and Kat's swift-witted ripostes will keep you chuckling as you discover the secrets they keep from each other, while unraveling a most perplexing intrigue.

SECOND CHANCE AT LOVE is pleased to introduce another new writer — Elizabeth Henry, author of *Man Trouble* (#277). Like other heroines you've met, Marcy has a low opinion of men — especially Rick Davenport, who climbs through her bedroom window after midnight and challenges her to all sorts of fun and games. But no other heroine must contend with an alter ego called Nosy, who butts in with unasked-for advice. Nonstop banter makes *Man Trouble* as light, crunchy, and fun to consume as popcorn.

In *Suddenly That Summer* (#278) by Jennifer Rose, Carrie Delaney's so fed up with the dating game that she spends a week at a tacky singles resort, determined to find a husband. But she's so busy participating in the toga party, forest scavenger hunt, and after-dark skinny dip that she refuses to recognize the man of her dreams — even when he insists he's "it"! Thank goodness James Luddington has the cleverness and persistence to win Carrie by fair means or foul. Finding a mate has never been so confusing — or so much fun!

In *Sweet Enchantment* (#279), Diana Mars employs warmth and skill to convey the joys and heartaches of combining two families into one through a new marriage. Pamela Shaw, whom you know as Barrett Shaw's sister-in-law in *Sweet Trespass* (#182), has to deal with her son's antagonism toward her new love, Grady Talliver, *and* with Grady's four young sons. But lizards in the bathroom, a bed sprayed with perfume, and a chamber of horrors in the attic don't ruffle our heroine, who more than adequately turns the tables on her little darlings. *Sweet Enchantment* is a story many of you will identify with — and all of you will enjoy.

Have fun!

Ellen Edwards

Ellen Edwards, Senior Editor
SECOND CHANCE AT LOVE
The Berkley Publishing Group
200 Madison Avenue
New York, N.Y. 10016

SWEET ENCHANTMENT

DIANA MARS

A SECOND CHANCE AT LOVE BOOK

SWEET ENCHANTMENT

Copyright © 1985 by Diana Mars

All rights reserved. No part of this publication may be reproduced or transmitted in any form or by any means, electronic or mechanical, including photocopy, recording, or any information storage and retrieval system, without permission in writing from the publisher.

Requests for permission to make copies of any part of the work should be mailed to: Permissions, Second Chance at Love, The Berkley Publishing Group, 200 Madison Avenue, New York, NY 10016.

First edition published July 1985

First printing

"Second Chance at Love" and the butterfly emblem are trademarks belonging to Jove Publications, Inc.

Printed in the United States of America

Second Chance at Love books are published by
The Berkley Publishing Group
200 Madison Avenue, New York, NY 10016

To everyone who asked
what happened to Pamela Shaw

Chapter 1

THE PLAINTIVE CRY of a sea gull rent the misty morning air. Pamela Shaw saw its unsteady flight in the sky before the bird once again crashed against damp, grainy cliffs, this time not attempting another takeoff. Pamela's innate compassion came to the fore, as she decided to put her medical training at the service of the sea gull. She turned off the main road leading to her lake property and careened onto a side road—only too late noticing the large shape emerging from a wooded area to her left. The figure headed right into the path of her Cavalier.

Pamela heard a sickening crunch and abandoned all thoughts of the injured sea gull as she slammed on the brakes and threw the car into stillness. Opening the door, she dived from the car and ran around it, to where a big man lay sprawled on the dirt road.

He had the physique of an Adonis, Pamela noted.

Even though it was still chilly in late May in northern Michigan, the man was shirtless, the wide expanse of his bronzed back uncovered, as were the long, muscular legs that gleamed in the sun from sweat and the golden mat of hair that decreased as it neared the top of his very brief, orange running shorts.

Her eyes, alert and trained, quickly took stock of the situation, even as she admired the man's physique. She saw that one leg was bent at an unnatural angle and her heart lurched. Not at the possibility of injury—she had a strong stomach and did not lose her head in an emergency—but at the fact that she was the cause of such an injury. And pain.

Even as Pamela knelt next to him, the man began to move. He turned first on his side; then, with considerable difficulty, he rolled onto his back. A moan, which he could not totally repress, accompanied his movements, and Pamela's hazel eyes filled with sympathy. His own gray gaze was glazed, and she saw him look at her metallic green car before his eyes came to rest on her.

"Cavalier. What an appropriate name for your style of driving."

The words were gritted out, and despite her concern, Pamela felt a surge of admiration for the man's nerve. It took a lot of courage and determination to joke at a time like this, when his face was twisted into a grimace of pain and beads of sweat poured out of him like a spring shower.

"I'm so sorry," she said finally, her voice husky with empathy and worry. The man tried to get up and groaned, falling back down. Just like the sea gull who had precipitated this unfortunate occurrence, Pamela thought. "Where does it hurt?" she asked him softly.

A throaty, dusky laugh emerged from the tanned throat. "Lady, where *doesn't* it hurt!" the stranger growled. He tried to sit up once more, and vividly cursed his inability to do so. "Could you help me get up," he demanded gruffly, "or are you the type to faint at the smallest drop of blood?"

Pamela hid a smile, forbearing to tell him she was a medical administrator at Northern General Hospital. "No, I'm not squeamish. But I think you should be careful. And I certainly don't want to do any more damage—"

"As long as you stay away from the wheel, we'll be okay," he barked. Pamela moved to kneel by his head and put her arm about his neck, trying to help him up. But he yelped as her fingers dug into his left shoulder. "Watch it!"

"Sorry," she said, smiling encouragingly. "Are you sure you don't want to wait for an ambulance?"

"And freeze before help arrives? Which, considering your driving record, is not a sure thing. With my luck, you'd be up a tree before you even reached the hospital."

Pamela wisely refrained from commenting on his metaphors or his negative attitude about her driving—which before today had earned safety citations. She lowered her hand to under his armpit and shoved—boy, was he heavy! Eventually, she succeeded in getting the mammoth chest into a vertical position.

The man did not look grateful, but Pamela couldn't really blame him. He must be in an awful lot of pain. She began to examine him, trailing her hands briskly from his powerful torso downward. The man gasped, remaining immobile for a second as she passed over the waistband of his shorts.

"What the hell do you think you're doing?"

Pamela shrank back, startled, and her hands dropped into his lap. Immediately, she felt flesh hardening beneath her fingers and drew her hands away.

"Is this your usual practice—disable men and then take advantage of them?"

Pamela's gaze flew up to meet his, and she whipped back the strands of soft, tawny hair from her face, as she always did when issued a challenge. But when she saw the mocking gleam in his gray eyes, she relaxed.

"There wouldn't be much point to it, would there?" she retorted. "I like my men able-bodied . . . and able."

His gaze conceded her this point and she continued her investigation, discovering no broken ribs or exceedingly serious damage. She announced, "You have a broken leg—"

"I could have told you that," he interrupted. Raising his left hand till it was under her small, straight nose, he added, "And a broken hand and sprained shoulder."

"Your wrist's only sprained—"

"Broken."

"Sprained. And your shoulder's bruised," she declared firmly. "I have an emergency kit. Let me get it and I'll put your leg in a temporary cast."

He was frowning when she returned and remained scowling while she attended to him.

"What about my left shoulder and wrist?" he demanded. "They're broken, too."

Pamela calmly shrugged her lilac shirt out of her wool violet slacks and tore a piece all around the hem.

"Your wrist's sprained and your shoulder bruised," she corrected, "but I'll put your arm in a sling." He winced as she did, and Pamela hid a smile. He'd been as stoic as an Indian while she'd tended his leg, but now was making a major production out of a mere sprained wrist. True, even a sprain could be painful, but she suspected the fair-haired stranger did not like to be wrong.

"What's your name, by the way?" she asked calmly as she wrapped the makeshift sling around his arm.

"Yes, you'll need it for the insurance forms," he told her nastily. Pamela leaned closer to him to tie a knot around his neck and grinned at him.

The grin seemed to infuriate him, and he grabbed her around the waist, which had felt cold as the lake wind had insinuated itself against her flesh. But she suddenly no longer felt cold.

"Kind of cocky, aren't you, for someone who's just run down an innocent pedestrian," he said gruffly.

"You're no innocent anything," Pamela said, still grinning. "I have apologized, but we must share the blame. You came out of the woods like a bat out of hell."

He frowned as he was reminded of his own culpability. "Perhaps," he admitted reluctantly. "But you're the driver. You're supposed to watch out for pedestrians. And I'm the one with the broken limbs."

"Limb," Pamela said, shaking her head. "And until now I've had no need to watch for anyone, since I've had no neighbors. But obviously, you can't be in too much pain, if you can sit here dallying about . . ."

"Dallying about!" His arm tightened about her waist. "You shouldn't push a man. I could be an escaped desperado intent on ravishing the first maiden I come upon."

"A desperado in Fila shorts and shoes? Besides, sorry to disillusion you, but I'm no maiden." Smiling, she ran one of her hands down to his leg and the other to the sprained wrist. "And you're certainly in no shape to ravish anyone."

An unwilling smile curved his wide, sensuous mouth at her thinly veiled warning. The gray eyes roved her body in a caress as warm as a summer wind.

"Totally heartless," he murmured, stroking her waist and letting the fingers of his right hand trail slowly up her back. "You don't even care that you've made me a cripple for a few weeks, incapacitating my hand and leg like this."

"Just be grateful it's your left side," Pamela said with deliberate flippancy. The hand against her back felt too good and too sure for comfort. She didn't think this man would have any trouble at seduction—even as a partial invalid. She pulled away, and after a slight hesitation, he let her go.

Pamela helped him up, reminding him she still didn't know his name.

"Grady Talliver."

He remained silent as they traversed the short distance to the passenger's side. Although no sound issued from him, Pamela knew Grady was in a lot of pain, and after he half hobbled, half leaned on her, he collapsed onto the seat.

Pamela took hold of both of his legs and set them carefully inside the car. Her eyes were inches away from his trim, hard midsection, and she once again saw a tenting within his tight shorts.

She backed up, unconsciously shaking her head, and Grady read her movement right. As she went to close the door on his side, he grinned and said, "Food and sex are our most powerful drives. I'm not hungry right now."

Speechless for once, Pamela slammed the door and went around to her side. As she settled behind the wheel, Grady said huskily, "Have pity on me, will you? I'm at your mercy."

Pamela couldn't help grinning, and was about to chastise him when she noticed how pale he looked. She'd seen people with broken bones whose pain diminished almost entirely once the bones had been set. But Grady also had a sprained wrist and bruised shoulder, and shock was setting in.

Putting her arm about his shoulder—careful of the injured side—Pamela pulled him toward her. "Lean against me," she instructed. "I don't have a blanket, and you're going to be shuddering."

"My pleasure," he murmured. Snuggling his big body against the softness of hers, Grady added, "Maybe being run down in the prime of life has its compensations."

As the first chill shook his muscular frame, Pamela floored the accelerator. Through chattering teeth, Grady muttered, "Do you own stock in race cars?"

His words were accompanied by a further burrowing against her gently rounded frame. His right hand took possession of her thigh. He was in an awkward position, having to favor his left side, but there was no need for those knowing digits to do any finger-walking.

Shifting her leg in an attempt to evade his seeking hand, Pamela told him sweetly, "I'm in a rush. When I ran into you, I was going to the aid of a sea gull. I have to hurry back to it."

Looking at her through eyes bright with fever, Grady asked in mocking incredulity, "You fly, too?"

Puzzled, she asked, "Fly?"

"You knocked him right out of the sky, right?"

Pamela grimaced, conceding him that one, then told him, "No, as a matter of fact the sea gull's not on my hit list."

"Lucky sea gull."

Another shudder rippled through his big frame, and Pamela instinctively raised her arm to touch his damp forehead, her cool fingers brushing away the straight golden hair adhering to it.

Hiding her worry, she negotiated a ninety-degree turn at hair-raising speed onto the main highway, taking them into town one-handed. "Sea gulls are safe from me," she told him, removing his hand, which had become an intolerable distraction. "I usually cruise around looking for a better target . . . an endangered species, the smart-mouthed, quick-handed macho male."

This time, Grady made the concession. "Touché," he said but the last syllable was swallowed up in another convulsion. Pamela pressed down still harder on the accelerator, and made full speed for the hospital.

Chapter

2

PAMELA WAS PROUD that Northern General was a progressive hospital. Unlike others she had worked in—as a candy striper while in high school, during her work-study program in X-ray technology, and later for her medical management degree—Northern General was not a utilitarian white. The different wards were decorated in various colors and themes, from the wild, vivid prints and animal motifs in the children's wing to the pinks and blues of the maternity ward to the restful soft green of recovery.

Now, as Pamela entered the parking lot at warp speed and screeched to a stop in front of emergency, she was also proud of her workplace for another reason: efficiency. As she gently pushed a shivering Grady away from her and ran to the other side to help him out, two male attendants were already slamming the emergency doors open in true TV-movie style and rushing forward to assist her.

But Grady refused the stretcher and help, muttering, "I can make it inside under my own steam."

One of the men, a stocky, brawny male nurse named Biff, frowned at Grady's stubbornness and asked, "Do you want us to carry him in, Ms. Shaw?"

One brown eyebrow quirked, Grady remarked, "You're obviously notorious. Do you get a percentage out of victims you send to the emergency room?"

"Not a bad idea. But I don't have to. Mulishness like yours will multiply your bills and raise the profit margin of Northern General."

Grady relented enough to let one of the male nurses help him by lifting his right arm and putting it over his own shoulder, as was done in war movies, but Pamela noticed with amusement that it was Ron who was allowed the privilege, not brawny, belligerent Biff.

As Pamela followed and Biff carried the portable stretcher, muttering under his breath about obstinate SOB's, Ron teased, "Are you starting a side business, Ms. Shaw?"

"I don't think the illustrious Doctor Phelps, would approve, Ron," she said, naming the head of the hospital. She winked at the younger man, who had applied to medical school and was anxiously awaiting an answer. Pamela had listened sympathetically to Ron's plans, fears, and aspirations, and shared a friendly, bantering relationship with him.

But Grady didn't know that, and as he turned his head and caught her wink, he said acerbically, "Robbing the cradle, Ms. Shaw?"

As they reached the waiting area, Pamela leaned forward to ease Grady's leg as Ron helped him into a seat. Looking up at the handsome young man, she asked him, "*Am* I robbing the cradle, Ron?"

Grady snorted in disgust, and Ron answered, his flashing dark eyes going from Grady to Pamela and back with amusement. "Not if you ask me. You have my permission to rob whatever you wish, Ms. Shaw."

Pamela walked over to the registering nurse and in a low voice quickly gave an account of what had happened. "Expedite things on Grady Talliver, Alice. He may be acting tough and difficult, but he's near collapse. He'll be staying overnight for observation, so I'll fill out his forms later." Alice nodded. As she was about to leave, Pamela added, "And don't tell him about me. I wouldn't put it past him to check himself out and come over to the house waving insurance forms."

"Okay, Pamela," Alice said. Then, in a louder tone, she told Grady, "Mr. Talliver, there are only two cases ahead of you. We should get to you within the next fifteen minutes."

"Take your time," Grady told her. "My assailant has a whole bunch of forms to fill out." Then, as he spied Pamela moving stealthily toward the exit, he straightened in his seat. "Where the hell do you think you're going? You're not getting off scot-free . . ."

His voice was raspy with a mixture of incredulity, anger, and pain. He tried to get up, but brawny Biff shoved him none too gently on his uninjured shoulder. "Hold it, mate. You're not going anywhere."

Pamela turned at the door, knowing she was leaving him in good hands, and waved cheerfully. "Be good, Mr. Talliver. You'll get excellent care here, if you cooperate. I have to tend to that sea gull."

As the wind caught the ragged ends of her blouse and flapped them against her midriff, her last view of Grady was of glazed gray eyes and sensually sculpted lips that mouthed "Sea gull?"

Rushing into the house, Pamela got a thick towel to wrap the sea gull in. It was lucky, she reflected, that the bird hadn't been successful in getting off the rock, or he'd have fallen into the lake and the waves would have battered his weakened body against the shore.

As she went into the kitchen, Pamela kept the gull nestled against her chest despite his very loud, discordant protests. When the strong beak began searching for a place to attack, Pamela folded the towel over his head and the indignant squawking increased.

After walking over to the green phone on the white and green wall, she dialed the hospital.

"Northern General ER," Alice said into the phone, her voice sounding as harried as usual.

"Hi, Alice. It's Pamela. Just checking on Mr. Personality."

Alice laughed and Pamela could picture her friend's blue eyes filled with mischief. In sixteen years as a nurse, Alice had seen a lot and could cope with just about every crisis devised by man or nature.

"Mr. Personality was livid when you traipsed off. Both Biff and Ron were needed to restrain him. You bagged yourself quite a hunk there."

"He's not *my* hunk," Pamela said, smiling. In the few weeks she'd been at Northern, some of the nurses had already made a concerted, strategic effort to liven up her love-life—Alice in particular. "Will he be all right?"

"Good as new in a couple of weeks. Dr. Kowalski said you did an excellent job, and the fact that you tended him on the spot will hasten his recovery. It's only a simple fracture."

"I'll bet Grady Talliver doesn't consider it simple," Pamela conjectured.

Alice chuckled. "Nope. He began issuing dire and dark threats against you and the hospital and the whole state of Michigan, but Stan shut him up, saying he had you to thank for a quicker than normal recovery. As it was, he was so furious with you, he hardly noticed the pain."

"Good," Pamela said, much relieved. "It makes me

feel better. After all, I did run the fellow down."

"Well, he's lucky it was you," Alice said loyally. "How's the sea gull?"

"He's angry, too," Pamela said, laughing. The bird was obviously feeling better also, now that he was out of the elements, nice and warm against her breast. His continued wriggling threatened to dislodge him from his safe perch.

"All men are alike under the skin—or feathers, in this case," Alice declared. "Unappreciative ingrates. Well, got to run, kiddo. See you tomorrow."

Pamela finished setting the tiny splint on the sea gull and put him on the windowsill, where he could see the trees, lake, and wildflowers outside, and the warm rays of the sun could reach him.

She stood back and regarded her patient warmly. Jonathan Livingston, she'd call him—J.L. for short. She'd always liked taking care of animals. When her parents had concentrated all their love on her older brother, Paul, she'd turned to pets and wild things for comfort.

Her eyes filled with tears. Inexplicably, seeing J.L. peer uncertainly at his surroundings, trying to get his bearings, looking at her with distrust, reminded her of her lonely, emotionally deprived childhood. Her parents had not been deliberately cruel. They had just wanted one child, and a boy at that. Having had their wish granted, they were somewhat taken aback when she showed up seven years later. They had done their duty by her, but all their love and affection and energies had gone into Paul. And Paul had been kind enough, but he'd been too old to have her tagging along. They'd never been close.

Then, later, her parents had disapproved of her marrying Trevor right after high school graduation, disapproving also when she became pregnant right away. When she was only four months pregnant with Eric, they had died in a boating accident in the Caribbean, and she'd had no support or maternal counsel in the trying, difficult months of her pregnancy.

Now Paul was settled in Nevada, and she'd left her life in Illinois, which she'd enjoyed, as well as her close relationship with Barrett, her brother-in-law, and his family. She'd left friends and a secure job and comfortable condominium in Schaumburg to start a new life in Michigan, as a hospital administrator. But she loved her new job, and the beautiful house on the lake which she'd always dreamed of. And she had her son Eric. What more could she ask for?

She brushed off the uncharacteristic moment of depression occasioned by her remembrance of a painful period in her past. After all, she was an optimist, and had always been able to pick herself up and go on. She'd always kept hope even through her difficult pregnancy when she was grieving over the death of her parents; even through Eric's infancy, when Trevor resented the demands motherhood made on her, something he obviously hadn't considered before his son was born. Through Trevor's jealousy, and later his infidelities, she'd always looked to a happier future.

And she'd never allowed herself to fall into another depression since getting back on her feet four years ago. In trying to be more of a wife, she'd become too little of a mother, and Eric had been hurt in the process. Not irretrievably, thank God. Both Trevor's brother, Barrett, and his wife, Helena, and their little girl, Corinna, had had a lot to do with Eric's fast recovery from his own depression and his father's neglect.

Now fourteen, Eric had been excited about moving to Michigan and having a place by the lake—even if he had been understandably sad about leaving his family and his friends. Remembering how a certain company—BNT—had wanted to purchase her land and build some kind of soccer camp on it, Pamela considered herself lucky that she had anticipated them by a few months. The Westons, the previous owners of her property, could probably have made a better deal with the conglomerate that had contacted her several times by phone and letter and had even sent out a Mr. Lewis to see her. But despite BNT's insistence and their representative's persuasiveness and generous offer, Pamela had not wanted to sell what she'd been looking for all her life.

Abruptly, Pamela realized that she'd been standing and daydreaming for quite a while with two tiny bowls in her hand. Moving cautiously so as not to startle the sea gull, she filled the bowls, one with water, the other food. Placing them carefully on the windowsill, she backed away.

J.L. stood indecisively for a bit, then condescended to look from the dishes to Pamela and back again. His beady, alert eyes gleamed suspiciously for a time longer, and when Pamela made no further move, the bird took a tentative hobble forward. Pamela smiled but stood absolutely still, watching with quiet triumph as J.L. essayed a downward movement, checked her out again, and, finally convinced it was safe, greedily bent his soft, mottled head to the feed dish.

Poor little thing, Pamela thought. So brave and determined to survive. When she'd finally gotten to the bird after a frantic dash to the bluffs, she had felt it might be too late. J.L. had been motionless, wet, cold. But that had facilitated her nursing. After she'd dried and warmed him up, and had treated his leg and wing, the sea gull had quickly revived. He was distrustful of her, but that was understandable. And although it was going to be nice to have him for company over the next ten days before Eric arrived from his Uncle Barrett's, Pamela did not want to domesticate him and perhaps threaten his subsequent survival. She merely wanted to restore him to health and then set him free.

As J.L. drank thirstily from the water dish, still keeping watch over her, Pamela walked toward the ancient refrigerator, another of the things she needed to replace in her last stages of furnishing the house. She opened the door of the refrigerator, which was a peculiar shade of green, and peered inside, looking for inspiration for tonight's solitary dinner.

The sudden, insistent ringing of the doorbell, which had been rigged to sound like cannons going off—Mr. Weston, the previous owner, had been a history buff—made J.L. screech and lose his precarious balance, and Pamela hit her head against the freezer handle.

Cursing eloquently, Pamela walked over to the sink to rescue poor J.L., who'd fallen into the bowl of freshly cut lettuce, tomato, and pickles. As she picked up the once-again terrified creature, holding him against her chest, Pamela could feel his little heart beat precipitously against his damp, downy breast.

Disgruntled, she stormed to the front door, intending to let the poor sucker have it. A vacuum cleaner she didn't need, or an encyclopedia or cosmetics, and she intended to tell the salesperson so. She'd been here only a few weeks, and no one ever came into this secluded area except for overly ambitious door-to-door salespeople.

Knowing the heavy oak door tended to stick, Pamela gave it a mighty shove.

And found herself jumping instinctively out of the way and staring dumbfounded at the breathing monolith that catapulted into her foyer.

She heard a startled, "What the hell—" in passing as her impromptu visitor half limped, half flew past her, unable to maintain his balance because of the heavy cast that had replaced her quick splinting job. Open-mouthed, she watched Grady Talliver land in her living room, bypassing the three steps as his momentum carried him right onto the oversize sofa, narrowly avoiding the large coffee table in his path through some agile, last-minute body twisting.

His crutches sailed in opposite directions, one crashing against the wall and dislodging a picture and the other miraculously missing the glass on the china cabinet in the adjoining dining room.

Grady's breath whooshed out of him as he landed face down, and Pamela winced as his cast made an ominous thump against the coffee table facing the sectional couch. But she was thankful for her latest arrangement of furniture, for if the couch had not been there she would have faced a total invalid, with both legs useless and perhaps a broken nose and broken arm to complete the ensemble.

As it was, Grady cursed a blue streak, then buried his face in the pearl-gray cushions and stuck his bottom in the air to negotiate a purchase on verticality.

And a nice bottom it was, too, Pamela thought as she soothingly stroked J.L. and approached Grady. It was small and tight, but not flat, she saw, the two well-rounded cheeks lovingly encased in dove-gray slacks that also fit perfectly around the crotch . . .

"Are you through checking out my endowments? Because if so, I could use some help straightening."

Being caught during her interested inspection caused Pamela's face to turn bright red. She swallowed sheepishly and raced forward, in her haste tripping over the steps Grady had sailed over.

"Oh, great! Miss Graceful Ballerina herself. Talk about the blind leading the blind."

By the time Pamela reached Grady, she was no longer mortified, having recovered her full composure. There had been a time when she'd been shy and somewhat insecure, but working in a hospital and supporting herself and her son had changed all that.

Resisting the urge to push Grady's face deeper into

the cushions, she extended a hand. "Here. I'll pull you up."

Grady turned his head another fraction of an inch and Pamela winced as she heard a distinct snap. "You thinking of pulling up one hundred and eighty-five pounds of disabled male with one dainty little hand?"

The dainty little hand clenched as Pamela set J.L. on an end table out of harm's way.

"How do you propose I unearth an uninvited male from my couch?"

"Come around and get under me."

Pamela moved closer and looked at the space between couch and male flesh. A tight fit.

"I don't think so. I'll just pull on your right arm—"

"And pull it out of its socket? No thanks," Grady said dryly. "I don't fancy total permanent disability."

Pamela frowned. "What about if I put my arms around your waist and pull?"

Grady shrugged his shoulders and winced. "Try it."

Pamela did, finding the proximity to recently bathed male, granite thighs, and firm buttocks more than a little disturbing. Why couldn't she see Grady Talliver as just another patient? He certainly was not the first handsome man she'd dealt with . . .

She hugged and puffed and tugged and puffed some more, but the massive frame did not go up. In the end, she had to admit defeat.

Could Grady be trying to sabotage her efforts?

"Well? Are you ready to have me add whiplash and a probably dislocated neck to my lawsuit?"

"Lawsuit?" Pamela repeated, dropping his waist as if it were burning bricks.

Grady managed to nod from his impossibly contorted position. "Better get moving, or you'll be counting popped vertebrae soon."

Thoroughly annoyed, yet a little apprehensive, Pamela sat on the edge of the couch.

"Hurry up, will you? And don't worry . . . I won't bite."

"Noble of you," Pamela muttered, and tucked her knees against her chin to get underneath Grady's bridged body.

"Come on, woman. Put your legs either around or between my thighs."

At the suggestive words, Pamela looked up and found herself staring right into dove-gray pools. She swallowed the lump of sensual tension and opted for putting her legs between Grady's braced, outstretched ones, careful of the one with the cast.

"All right, now, push," he instructed as she was positioned right beneath him.

She tried, arching her body against his black silk shirt. But as she also had to be careful of the sling around his left arm, all that she accomplished was to rub her breasts, thinly clad in a lime eyelet blouse, against Grady's powerful chest. And she could have sworn his left arm, restrained as it was, managed to caress her right breast.

But when she looked up again, she saw a pair of gray eyes that betrayed no knowledge, no awareness, of their close contact. Determined to be just as indifferent, Pamela pushed harder, but all she succeeded in doing was to force Grady's right leg to bend under his weight. As it was dislodged, he toppled forward like a felled tree.

He had fallen into her lap!

Chapter 3

PAMELA GASPED AS the breath was knocked out of her body in one big rush, and Grady said complacently, "Well, you've finally got what you wanted."

"Wh–what *I* wa-wanted?" Pamela wheezed out.

"Sure. You've got a disabled man in your clutches—or in your lap, to put it precisely."

As his right arm was braced against the couch, ostensibly to prevent him from crushing her beyond recognition, Pamela protested adamantly, "I don't want you in my lap . . . or anywhere. Now get off me."

"Tsk, tsk. A maniacal driver, a dishonest hit-and-runner, and now a hypocrite, to boot. What am I to do with you?"

Beginning to worry, Pamela looked into the gray eyes for any signs of shock, fever, or drug overdose. After all, what did she really know of this man, a total stranger? And he'd not only managed to barge into her house, unannounced and uninvited, but was even now covering her body with his own!

"I am not a maniac. I have safety citations—" she began, building her defense.

"From the Road Runner company?"

"And I did not hit and run—"

"You left without giving me your name and address or that of your insurance company—if you even have one. And the nurse you talked to would divulge only her own name, rank, and serial number."

"And I am not a hypocrite," Pamela finished her side of the disjointed conversation. Gaining strength and self-assurance from righteous indignation, she said, "Now, will you please get off? Because if you make your living by suing people, let me tell you, you'll soon find nothing left to sue but a badly mangled corpse."

Grady shifted a little so she could get some air into her deflated lungs, but his thighs tightened around hers.

"Character-wise, I'd say you're on the debit side, but personality and figure-wise, you're on the credit side. A lopsided but interesting equation."

Pamela could hear the birds chirping outside in the slow-gathering darkness, the symphony of waves on shore, and she could smell the distinctive scent of Irish Spring and warm, aroused male. This last cleared her own brain of its lingering vestiges of confusion, and she checked the reins on her own unbridled response and consequent alarm.

"I don't like rating games, Mr. Talliver. Or dating games, for that matter. Now either you get off me or I start pounding on your injured arm until you do."

Grady's eyes narrowed, and then he moved with incredible speed. Before she could anticipate his action and counter it, he had grabbed one hand, and then the other, holding both of her wrists in one strong, broad hand, which he raised over her head.

Her hazel gaze followed his as it dropped to her bustline, and she noticed with dismay how her soft breasts, daintily covered by a lace and satin bra, had strained against the thin material of her blouse until one pearl button had popped open, revealing a small satin butterfly.

The way her distended nipples tingled under his visual assault told her she was not really afraid of Grady Talliver. Her instincts had always guided her, and she'd never feel arousal for a man who evoked fear in her.

As she suspected, he was not as disabled as he'd led her to believe. His quick response and easy strength had demonstrated that.

As his eyes held hers, he murmured, "Shouldn't telegraph your intentions."

Pamela attempted to free her hands, not liking the feeling of being helpless, and she looked him straight in the eye as she said, "If you're really in that dire a need, I can direct you to the proper section of town. As a matter of fact, I'll even drive you there."

His brow furrowed and he looked at her suspiciously. "What are you talking about?"

"Merely that if your social graces leave a lot to be desired, or if you've been celibate too long, I can point you in the right direction."

"You keep names of friendly hookers on hand, do you?" he asked, amused.

Pamela felt the relaxation in him, and as he let go of her hands retorted. "They're in the business. I'm not."

"I'm sure they appreciate your sending clients their way, but I prefer to choose and chase my quarry."

Pamela remembered her earlier statement in the car, and knew he did, too. He smiled, and Pamela could not help responding.

His head lowered, and for a moment Pamela thought that he meant to kiss her. But then his thick brown lashes dropped to guard his expression, and he pushed away so she could breathe easier and their upper torsos were barely touching.

"You're cruising for endangered species, and I'm temporarily out of commission . . ."

"Not completely," Pamela retorted.

"So you'll just have to nurse me back to health before you can hunt me down."

"You don't need me to help you in the seduction department. You were doing quite well on your own."

"Oh, then you don't think my social graces are beyond repair?"

Pamela whipped her head sideways to get the heavy wave of hair out of her left eye. "I was speaking hypothetically. Your seductive scheme was quite imaginative, and might have been successful if there had been a susceptible female around."

"It wasn't entirely a scheme. I really cannot get off this couch unaided."

"But you did take advantage of the situation."

"I'm a businessman. I maximize potential and try to find a positive side to everything." His grin showed a dazzling array of even white teeth. "Besides, it was good practice for your nursing me." Ignoring her indignant gasp, he asked, "Shall we try together?"

As they both worked to get his body turned and up, Pamela groaned. "I've told you, you don't *need* a nurse. My being on the scene of the accident—"

"Scene of the crime, you mean," he snorted as they almost had him standing. But not quite.

"We'll have you walking quite soon. I know quite a bit about broken bones—"

"No doubt from practical experience—"

"And yours was a simple fracture. If you stop flying into people's homes, and stumbling indiscriminately about, you ought to be walking in a couple of weeks. You're young—" She shoved upwards as Grady pulled, and they both lost their balance, Pamela's head hitting

Grady's chin resoundingly as she was finishing, "And you have a strong constitution."

"Not anymore," Grady said lugubriously. Rubbing his reddened chin, he added, "Definitely whiplash."

"Oh, for heaven's sake, let's coordinate this and get it over with!"

After another attempt, they pushed and pulled together, and finally succeeded in getting Grady vertical.

As they both stood, breathing hard and covered with a light film of perspiration, Grady threw his coup de grâce at her.

"I have great confidence in my marvelous knitting powers, and Northern General's healing powers—despite the fact that some of the staff seem to be on friendly terms with a drag racer—but you're forgetting one thing."

"Jonathan Livingston!" Pamela cried.

"Jonathan Livingston?" Grady repeated blankly.

Pamela felt his puzzled eyes on her as she raced toward the end table and saw it empty of J.L. With a sinking heart, she was afraid the sea gull might have gotten too near the two flailing bodies or the cast and been crushed underneath during their gargantuan struggle.

But she spotted him in the arched, carved doorway between living room and dining room, looking as indignant and neglected as a bird can possibly look. She picked him up, and this time he didn't try to take a bite out of her as she moved around the room retrieving Grady's crutches.

She walked over to Grady and handed them to him, and he said, "I don't have much use for two of them. My left arm hurts like the very devil."

"Oh, I'm sorry," Pamela said, concerned. "Do you have any painkillers with you?"

"Yes, I do. But my problem is that I won't be able to use my left hand for a few days."

"Then you shouldn't tussle with strange women on their couches. That will tend to aggravate things." She headed for the kitchen, intent on putting J.L. in a large carton now that the sun was almost gone. Grady followed her. "Besides," she continued airily, "you still have your right leg and arm. You said you were a businessman—you can still use your pen or computer or calculator, whatever it is you use—with your right hand."

"There speaks the voice of ignorance," Grady told her softly.

Pamela pivoted, ruffling J.L.'s feathers with her abrupt movement, and feeling her own ruffled, too, at his statement.

Running her hand softly over the squawking bird, Pamela was about to open her mouth when he anticipated her.

"Your prejudice is showing." He grinned with teeth that alarmingly resembled a shark's. "You're assuming I'm right-handed, as all right-handers are wont to do. But I'm a southpaw."

As Pamela prepared dinner, she did a silent, slow burn. Of all the underhanded, unscrupulous stunts . . . Of all the rotten luck, to run over a left-handed . . . left-handed . . . skunk . . .

Grady had wasted no time moving in when she had reluctantly—and somewhat guiltily—agreed to tend to his needs over the next few days. His rather spectacular entrance had momentarily obscured the fact that he'd had a fully packed suitcase outside.

Grady Talliver had even had the unmitigated gall to ask her when dinner was ready, as he announced he was quite ravenous. He'd even gone so far as to cheerfully volunteer his preferences, which ran to sushi, liver, and fried pork chops, all of which Pamela personally abhorred.

Now, as she fiercely sliced the potatoes for french fries—Grady had said he preferred mashed potatoes with oodles of gravy—she could hear the powerful strains of classical music, when she'd have much preferred some fast rock to chop by.

As she was cutting the last potato, Grady's stumbling entrance into the kitchen startled both Pamela, who knocked some of the potatoes with her elbow, and J.L., onto whose unsuspecting crown the sliced potatoes and parings descended.

"Poor J.L.," Pamela cried, rushing to the rescue as the sea gull's screeches increased in volume. She could hear human screeching and swearing in back of her, but at this moment she could not spare any sympathy for a man who had planted himself in her living room and demanded personal nursing care.

As she cleaned up the box into which the pieces of potato had fallen, the human squawking at her back asked, "Do you have to put obstacles in my path?" He put the stepladder to one side, and added in an offended tone, "Or are you trying to finish what you started this morning?"

Pamela grabbed some more paper towels and pulled angrily. Naturally, the dispenser came away in her hand and started flying, until a quick masculine hand stopped its fast trajectory.

"I couldn't reach the top shelf," she explained as Grady handed her the paper-towel dispenser. "So I had to use the stepladder to reach what I needed."

"You could have asked me to reach for it, or you could have put the ladder away afterward. I'm beginning to feel as if this house is a mine field."

Pamela gently dried an angry J.L. and said coolly, "I'm not about to ask you for anything. I didn't put the ladder there on purpose, and I certainly didn't ask you to invade my home." The absurdity of the situation began to get the better of her, but still she strove to keep her expression severe. "If you find my home too dangerous and obstacle-ridden, you can leave right now. The sooner the better."

"You still have papers to complete and sign—"

"Oh, for heaven's sake!"

"And my shoulder hurts. As well as my chin, my neck, my knee, and now my toe."

Grady looked down at his freshly stubbed toe, and Pamela had to suppress the chuckle tickling the back of her throat at the sight of a reddened big toe peeping out from a leather sandal.

"All right, all right. Let me take care of J.L.—"

Grady simultaneously cursed and limped, trying to favor both his toe and casted leg. "Here, let me help."

"No, thanks. You've scared him out of his wits enough for one night. Let's hope he doesn't have a weak heart."

"I know just how he feels," Grady declared wryly. He leaned against the sink as Pamela checked the sea gull's leg and wing. "I sure wish you'd use some of that tender loving care on me."

"J.L.'s totally blameless. And *he* hasn't accused me of lacking character or performing nefarious deeds."

"I'm giving you a chance to redeem yourself," he said. Pamela snorted. As she straightened after cleaning a bit of potato that had adhered tenaciously to J.L.'s soft throat, Grady added, "You missed one."

Holding on to the sink for balance, he bent and aimed for the little piece of potato skin on the bird's beak. Pamela cried, "Watch out!" just as J.L. lunged toward the—to him—threatening stranger.

Grady rescued his finger and showed it to her. "Still intact."

Pamela couldn't help but respond to his grin, and he asked, "What does J.L. stand for?"

"Jonathan Livingston—Seagull."

"Should have guessed."

"I liked the movie," Pamela challenged defensively.

"So did I. We must have been among the few who did."

Pamela moved the box to a corner, and replaced the

stepladder in a closet near the porch door. "Neil Diamond's album did well."

"Something had to. The critics lambasted the movie."

"I know. It was a weird film, but it had a kind of strange fascination to it, nonetheless."

"Just like you," Grady said dryly. "You mow me down, you run out on me, and then you have me pirouetting through your house. And I keep coming back for more."

"Can I help it if you're none too graceful and don't look where you're going? Besides—"

"I know, I know. I can leave anytime." As Pamela looked at him hopefully, he added blithely, "But I still need help. You immobilized me, so you'll have to be my right—or in this case, left—hand for a while."

He turned to leave the kitchen, this time looking about him exaggeratedly for any booby traps, and Pamela felt less exasperated about his presence. She was still not entirely happy, but she was willing to help the man out for a couple of days to allay the slight sense of guilt that still nagged at her.

"Uh, Mr. Talliver?"

He turned and put one hand on the doorway for balance. "Call me Grady, please. We've been through too much together to use last names."

Pamela's lips twitched, and she said, "Listen, I know you said you liked mashed potatoes. I made french fries, but there are still a few minutes until the breaded veal's ready, so I can whip you up some mashed potatoes if you like—"

"Don't bother. I hedged my bet. I like french fries, too, but I figured you wouldn't make them if I asked."

"Why, you lying, conniving . . ." Pamela said, laughing, and looked for an appropriate object to throw at him. She picked a plastic pineapple that had belonged to a centerpiece the Westons had left behind, but Grady didn't even duck.

He met the oncoming projectile with a graceful toss

of his head, and the pineapple came flying back at her like a boomerang.

"I'll have to teach you soccer some time." As Pamela looked for another object to pitch, he added over his shoulder as he hobbled away, "If I live long enough."

Chapter 4

"YOUR BROTHER?" GRADY asked as he sat down on a comfortable armchair, his foot propped on an ottoman, and looked at the photograph of a laughing boy on the end table.

Pamela gave him his pre-dinner drink. He'd insisted on having one, saying that he didn't intend to take any more painkillers; he didn't want to take the potent drugs unless absolutely necessary.

She smiled at the picture. "That's Eric, my son. He's fourteen now, and he's staying with my brother-in-law and his family in Illinois."

Grady's gaze went from the picture to her as she sat down on the couch, and he said, "I guess there's a slight resemblance . . ."

Pamela laughed. "No need to be polite. Eric looks like his father, except for the red hair. That's Barrett's."

Her voice had softened at the mention of her brother-in-law. Grady asked dryly, "I was worried for a moment there about a husband, but from your expression I must worry about Barrett—whoever he is."

"My brother-in-law," Pamela answered, her eyes lighting up with affection and wistfulness as she remembered her family back in Illinois.

"You did mention he had a family?"

"He married and acquired a delightful daughter, Corinna. He and his wife, Helena, are thinking of adding to the family one of these days."

"And you? Are you married? Or carrying a torch for redheaded Barrett?"

Pamela looked up, surprised at Grady's tone of disapproval. She detected disgruntlement, and yes, jealousy, in his gray eyes.

Hiding a smile, she said dreamily, "Actually, Barrett's hair is a gleaming shade of mahogany, and he has the bluest eyes this side of an ocean . . ."

"You're lusting after your brother-in-law?" His incredulous eyes went to her ringless finger and he asked belligerently, "And are you married or not? You're not wearing a ring."

Pamela met his accusing gaze and told him softly, "A bit late in the day for you to worry about it, wouldn't you say? After barging in here and demanding free medical assistance . . ."

"That was before I knew about Eric, and—"

"Oh?" she asked him as he waved toward her son's photograph. "You don't like boys, Mr. Talliver? Or is it just children in general?"

Grady smiled at her bristling tone and told her softly. "Oh, I like children all right. It's lurking lovers I disapprove of." At her raised eyebrows, he told her, "I have four of my own."

"Four lovers?"

His grin widened. "Four boys."

Pamela almost dropped her Cherry Kijafa. "You have four boys?" she repeated, stunned. Grady looked and acted like the quintessential bachelor—not a care or responsibility in the world.

"Yep. Ages twelve, ten, nine, and seven. They're staying with my parents in Ohio."

"I see." She really didn't, but she was a little dazed by his disclosure. Four sons! She sipped the dry, maroon-hued drink absently. She was about to ask Grady why the boys weren't with him, and where he lived, since he'd popped out of nowhere, when he posed a question of his own.

"You haven't answered yet. Are you married?"

Pamela crossed her legs and his eyes followed the long line of well-turned limbs, which working in the hospital had strengthened and toned.

"No, I'm divorced." She lowered the hem of her forest-green skirt past her knees and added, "My ex-husband lives in Georgia."

"He never sees your son?"

"Oh, he's better now. There was a time when Eric was at the bottom of his priorities, but now Trevor either comes to Illinois or has Eric fly out a few weekends every year, and tries to have Eric stay with him for at least three weeks in the summer." Putting down the smoke-colored glass on the carved end table, she asked, "What about your wife? Is she—"

"She's dead." Grady kept his voice even, but Pamela could still see the pain of loss in the shuttered gray gaze.

"I'm sorry," she said sincerely. "It must be hard," she added sympathetically. "At least with divorce, it's a personal choice, and these days usually a mutual one."

"You are a nice woman," Grady said unexpectedly.

Just as unexpectedly, Pamela felt the prickle of tears burning at her eyelids. "Why, for empathizing? We've all experienced the anguish of losing loved ones . . ."

"For much more than that," Grady said. "For caring, and giving of yourself—whether it's to a bird or a human."

Embarrassed, Pamela tried to make light of it. "You mean you no longer think I'll gyp you out of your insurance coverage?"

He smiled. "I haven't thought that for quite a while. I guess I'm going to end up thanking you for striking me down."

"Oh, come on. I feel guilty enough about that—"

"And I've cooled down enough to see that I was just as much to blame. But as I said, I'm mighty glad we've met. To have the pleasure of having a beauty with big hazel eyes, a kissable mouth, and a luscious figure nurse me, take care of all my needs . . ."

"I don't feel *that* guilty," Pamela said, and Grady laughed, a gritty sound that emanated from deep within his chest and did funny things to her own. "I'll see about dinner," she told him briskly, heading toward the kitchen, which adjoined the dining room.

"Can I help?" Grady said, starting to get up.

"Not tonight," Pamela answered. "I'll fix a chair in the kitchen tomorrow and you can help with the dishes, but for tonight you've had enough motion and commotion."

"Amen," Grady said solemnly, and Pamela shook her head, chuckling at his irrepressible humor.

Later that evening, as they sat down to dinner, Pamela asked, "How did you get out of Dr. Kowalski's clutches? You really should have stayed overnight in case of a possible concussion and any complications that might have set in."

"I don't particularly like hospitals or doctors or medications. I'm not against medicine, per se, only overusing medication. I prefer to let the body heal itself." Grady served himself more french fries and suddenly looked up. "How did you know I was accosted by a big gorilla named Kowalski?" His wide forehead knitted into a frown as he said, "Come to think of it, he seemed to know quite a bit about you. He chewed me out and told me what a good job you'd done, helping me bypass a week or two of recovery."

"Dr. Kowalski is one of the best, despite his gruff manner."

"Gruff? I thought the man was a displaced lumberjack, mistaking my leg for a tree trunk, the way he handled my limbs." His eyes narrowed, "There you go again. How come you know so much about these people? How well do you know Kowalski and that tight-lipped nurse? Is this some sort of conspiracy?"

Pamela served herself more wine and filled Grady's glass. "Actually, I know them quite well. I did tell you I knew something about bones."

Grady had stopped eating and looked at her with an expectant air. Pamela savored the moment. "I was an X-ray technician." Grady closed his eyes fatalistically, obviously guessing what was coming next. "And then I decided to get a degree in medical administration. I'm the hospital administrator at Northern General."

Grady smiled sheepishly and said, "Guess it's my turn to apologize."

"No need," Pamela said, laughing. "Your face said it all, and it was well worth it."

"You said your boy is in Illinois?" Grady turned the conversation casually as he resumed eating.

"That's right. I had a terrific job opportunity here in Michigan, but I didn't want Eric to leave school before the end of the term. By staying on with Barrett and Helena for a while, he was able to finish his freshman year with the rest of his class, and will have the chance to attend all the end-of-year/beginning-of-summer parties."

"You don't find this house too isolated?" Grady asked, his eyes meeting hers over the flicker of candlelight. To avoid raising their voices, they'd sat facing each other across the width of the table, rather than at the ends.

Pamela frowned, puzzled at the new switch of subjects.

"No, I love it here. It's exactly the kind of spot I want—away from the city, in the fresh air, near a lake. On this side of town there's only one other house, a few acres away. But I haven't met the neighbors who share the lake with me. I understand the old Jentzen house was purchased a couple of weeks ago, when I was away. I had a three-day weekend coming, and drove to Illinois to see Eric."

"Well, it certainly has been an evening of surprises," Grady said thoughtfully.

"Mmm," Pamela agreed absently, thinking again of the company that had approached her during Easter break when she'd come to bring the first of her belongings to her new house. She'd interviewed for her position at Northern General at Christmastime and had first seen the house then. She'd bought it a few weeks later. But those people from BNT had sure been persistent, to the point of sending a representative to try to convince her to sell. Mr. Lewis had certainly been a master of the soft-sell tactic. And the numerous letters and phone calls she'd received since . . .

"Still here?"

Grady's amused voice cut through her reveries, and Pamela looked up, smiling at him vaguely.

"Yes, I'm still here. I was just thinking of this company, BNT, which has been after me to sell my land."

Grady's body stiffened, and his gaze grew cautious. "Oh? And you don't want to sell?"

"I just bought it," Pamela said. "Of course I don't want to sell. This is a good place for Eric and me."

"But if they're offering a good price . . ." Grady ventured.

Pamela waved her hand impatiently, forgetting she was still holding her glass of wine. It sloshed perilously close to the rim, but luckily it was two-thirds empty, so the dark liquid did not splash onto the lace tablecloth.

"That doesn't matter. All of us have a nebulous idea of what the ideal place would be. I'm lucky enough to have actually found my dream spot, so I don't intend to move."

She sipped some more of her wine and set the glass down. Grady had a preoccupied air, and Pamela noticed how pale he was looking. Obviously, the repeated shocks of the day plus the unalleviated pain of his injuries, were taking their toll even on such a sturdy constitution as his.

Chastising herself for having let dinner be so prolonged when the man across from her was tired and hurting, she said softly, "Let's hope tomorrow is a peaceful, quiet day. I don't think either of us can stand any more surprises, do you?"

Grady seemed to turn a peculiar shade of green, and Pamela decided his arm and leg must be throbbing hellishly.

"Would you care for some dessert?" she offered, though she felt that Grady should really get to bed right away.

He shook his head and gave her a lopsided grin. When she got up to clear the table, he awkwardly attempted to stand also. Pamela waved him down. "I'll do it. Your face is starting to match your eyes."

"Thanks," Grady said wryly. "Actually, there *is* something else we haven't discussed."

Pamela tensed wearily. "I told you my insurance will cover—"

He waved her statement away. "It's about my business. I have a lot of work to catch up on."

"I'll help you when I get back from the hospital tomorrow."

"That's just the point. You can't go back to the hospital."

"I can't?" Pamela asked blankly.

"Not for a while. It's hard for me to get around, and the whole point of my staying here is so you can nurse me. How can you do that if you're away all day?"

Pamela's spine stiffened. "I do have a job, you know."

"But I need care."

"Check into the hospital."

"And take a bed away from someone who really needs it? I just need a private nurse."

"I'm not a nurse."

"But you know broken bones. And you caused mine. It's your responsibility to see that they're properly mended."

Pamela felt as if her back were about to snap in two. "That was a low blow."

Grady leaned back in his chair and smiled complacently. "Can I help it if my good side's immobilized? You even had to cut my meat for me. I'm as helpless as a baby."

Pamela's eyes slitted and she said with conviction, "*You* were never a baby. You were born a full-grown hustler."

"So you'll stay home for a couple of weeks?" Grady asked agreeably, pressing his advantage. He knew he had her by reawakening her slumbering conscience. The con artist! No wonder he was a businessman. And no doubt he was a very rich one, with aspirations to politics.

"I can't take two weeks off. Maybe a day or two."

"Or three of four? I really am in pain."

She didn't doubt it. His complexion was ashen, and perspiration beaded his forehead and upper lip. But he was really a low form of life to take advantage of her this way.

She told him so.

"You're lower than an earthworm, but I've never been able to stand seeing anything in pain. Not even you," she added reluctantly, going to his side and leaving the dishes for later, after she had him resting.

"I was counting on that," Grady told her confidently. But he had to grit his teeth as he leaned on her while she led him to one of the bedrooms.

"And here I was starting to like you—or at least, not dislike you so," Pamela muttered as she helped him traverse the dining room and hall leading into the back of the house.

"You'll like me, you'll see. Eventually, you'll even thank me."

Pamela laughed, equal parts of disbelief and affront in her mirth. "Let's get you into bed before you find yourself with another broken limb."

"You're too softhearted," Grady said contentedly as she helped him lie down on the king-size bed.

Pamela fixed the pillow under his head, then placed pillows under his arm and leg and was about to leave the blue and gold room when Grady said, "My clothes."

Pamela stopped and turned slowly. "What about them? Your got into them in the first place."

"I had the manager of the motel help me after I took a shower. And I was under the influence of painkillers then."

About to suggest more painkillers, Pamela recalled what he'd said about his reluctance to use them and mumbled instead, "All right. Let's get it over with."

She carefully took the sling off and then his black shirt, which had been fitted over the bandages. Then she helped him with the slacks, allowing him to open his silver buckle and zipper and then pulling off the gray pants, which he'd cut on one side to fit over the cast.

"Pity about the slacks," she commented.

"They can be replaced. I don't have any more spare parts," Grady told her shortly.

Pamela knew his temper arose partly out of his pain and partly out of pique. She'd acted coolly and professionally, and apparently Grady had expected her to drool over his body.

She inspected it quickly as he tried to get comfortable in bed, and liked the masculine geometry of wide shoulders and developed biceps tapering to a narrow waist, flat belly, and long, muscular legs. The dark gray briefs that molded his manhood left little to the imagination, but Pamela was not about to let any deep, heaving breaths escape her constricted chest at sight of his raw, virile beauty.

Instead, she stifled a yawn as she covered him with the navy comforter and surreptitiously stole another appreciative glance at his gorgeous body from under her thick golden-brown lashes.

"Need anything else?"

"Do I," Grady said, his voice and gaze full of smoldering meaning. Blast! Pamela thought. He could still be sexy as hell even half under the weather.

"Hot milk okay? Or would you prefer hot cocoa?"

His expletive left her in no doubt as to his opinion of those suggestions.

"How about some company?" he suggested throatily, but Pamela could see he was fading rapidly.

"J.L.?" she asked brightly. "Now there's a thought. I'll go get his box, but make sure he doesn't get near your fingers—"

Grady used the last of his quickly waning energy to lift his head from the pillow. "You bring that bird in here and I'll pluck him! He's caused me more misery, the treacherous, vicious scavenger..."

The deep masculine voice faded to a faint burr, then quieted altogether.

Pamela rearranged his arm more comfortably on the pillow, raised the covers to his chin, and looked for a moment into his rough-hewn features. The lashes curving like crescents on his prominent cheekbones looked all the darker against the temporary pallor of his skin. Turning the lamp off, she tiptoed out, although she had the feeling that nothing short of an earthquake would wake Grady before morning.

Chapter 5

THE NEXT MORNING Pamela checked on Grady, and saw that he was sleeping the slumber of the conscienceless.

Which was really an adequate way to describe the self-assured, blackmailing hunk currently occupying the spare bedroom, she thought, grinning.

She'd heard him moan during the night, when she'd kept vigil to make sure there were no signs of concussion or any complications. But exhaustion and delayed shock had overridden the actual hurt of his injuries and had prevented him from waking up.

She pinned him to the bed by tightening the sheets and cover around him, and securing them under the mattress. This way, Grady would find it hard to move and would have to wake up before rolling on his side accidentally.

Pamela put a glass of orange juice and a pitcher of

ice water on the nightstand for Grady, pushed the night-stand closer to the bed, and then quickly left the house.

The drive to the hospital was swift and reviving. Although not a morning person, Pamela had accustomed herself to function under any kind of schedule. Hospital work demanded it, and she liked the twenty-minute drive in fresh, scented air that allowed her to regain her full, functioning faculties. In wintertime, the trip to Northern General would take longer, but after living in Illinois, she was used to snow and enjoyed driving in it—as long as there was not a full-fledged blizzard.

It was ten to seven when she arrived at the hospital, but Pamela was sure that Royce Phelps would be there already.

He was. Dr. Phelps was not only a workaholic but also a dedicated physician. And he was a compassionate, understanding person, too.

This he demonstrated again by approving Pamela's request for the rest of the week off. When she promised to work the following weekend to make up the time lost this Thursday and Friday, he assured her it would not be necessary.

By ten o'clock, Pamela was ready to go home. She took with her some files that were too urgent to put off, intending to catch up on paperwork that the medical bureaucratic mill seemed to subsist on. She was not about to waste the next four days of enforced nursing.

The drive home was even quicker than the drive to the hospital, for Pamela encountered no traffic on the eastern side of town at ten in the morning. As she got out of the car, she decided to check on Grady to see if he was awake and needed something, but she found her answer as soon as she stepped into the house.

"Pamela! Is that you?"

She closed the door and nimbly took the steps into the recessed living room, pausing to drop her briefcase and folders on the couch.

She headed toward the rear of the house, and heard a loud, exacerbated roar.

"Pamela!"

She stepped into the bedroom and saw Grady tangled in the sheets and comforter, his face flushed from exertion and frustration, his eyes bright with fever.

"Where the hell have you been? I've been yelling for you for the past hour."

His voice, naturally low and gritty, sounded like sandpaper now, testifying to the veracity of his statement.

"I had to go into the hospital to arrange for a few days off," she informed him briskly.

As he attempted to get out of bed once more, his wide chest looking powerfully masculine and golden in the diffuse light of the room, Pamela walked toward her impromptu guest.

"Couldn't you have done it over the phone?" he asked her as she reached him.

"No. There are other people who are also hurt. I may not be a nurse or doctor, but medical facilities also need administrators in order to function without coming to a complete halt over finances, scheduling, or personnel acquisition. I not only had to get permission, but I also had to pick up some work."

"And in the meantime left me to fend for myself," he said accusingly.

"I hate to break this to you, but you're in no grave danger. Besides, if you were hurting a lot, you should have taken a pain pill. I left them right here by the pitcher." She began pouring him some ice water, but his brief expletive stopped her. "Not thirsty?" she asked, frowning. Surely, he must be; his fever had risen.

"I'm drier than a cactus, but I can't hold any more water in at the moment. I'm about to burst."

Pamela understood. "You need my help to get to the bathroom."

Grady attempted to get up once more, but his body failed him. Pamela knew he was still suffering from the aftershocks of the accident, and not taking the painkillers was certainly not helping his cause.

But now was not the time to take him to task, not when he was so obviously in pain. She thought he also seemed embarrassed.

Briskly, she put her arm about his waist and said, "Come on, I'll help you get to the bathroom. You can proceed from there on your own."

She had joked to relieve the tension, expecting a quick comeback. But just as Grady did not make a pass at her with such a golden opportunity, he also did not offer a witty rejoinder.

She now knew Grady *was* embarrassed. She tried to hide a smile, knowing that although men were normally less shy than women when talking about sex and displaying their bodies, they were definitely more ill at ease when discussing sicknesses, pregnancy, or when faced with something that they saw as lessening their masculine prowess or a threat to their ego.

Grady noticed her smile, though, and scowled at her. "What's so funny? Are you enjoying having me at your mercy?"

Stopping so he could lean against the bathroom doorway, Pamela faced him squarely. "I was just reflecting on the relative embarrassment thresholds of men and women. Women feel more awkward about expressing their sexual preferences and telling men what feels good to them, but men are equally uncomfortable when reproduction is discussed."

Her ploy succeeded. Grady straightened somewhat, his arm still about her, his earlier embarrassment forgotten.

"Reproduction. That's an interesting subject. Did sex enter your mind when you entered the bedroom?"

"I thought you had to go in a hurry," she parried, removing his hand from her body. It certainly felt good against her flesh, even through the layer of blouse and vest, but Grady needed to get well. Any extracurricular activity would not help his recovery process.

Despite her efforts to keep her cool, she could feel a slight tinge of warmth in her cheeks. Damn the man! She thought she'd grown very sophisticated and blasé in her volunteer work and classes, but being physically attracted to the man one was supposed to nurse put a different complexion on things.

And he knew it. And was taking advantage of it.

And she couldn't reproach him for it because she'd laid herself wide open for that kind of talk by initiating the subject of sex herself. From trying to set *him* at ease, they'd progressed to putting *her* on the defensive.

"You're turning a nice shade of pink," Grady said, his gray eyes taking in the conflicting, fleeting expressions on her face.

"And how nice of you to say so," she told him sweetly. "And now, if you'll excuse me, I'll get to work on lunch and my files. I'm sure you can manage to get back to bed on your own."

As she was about to turn away, Grady grabbed her by the shoulder with his right hand and spun her around.

"I'm sorry. I've been a heel. Here you were trying to erase my discomfort, and I've managed to unsettle you."

"The unsettling has very little to do with bodily functions," she told him, liking him more for having admitted his own self-consciousness. "I'm afraid that in the best of circumstances, men and women cannot help the sparks that fly between them. But they can and should control them."

He smiled with great satisfaction. "Then you *do* admit some attraction to me."

She quickly looked him up and down. "I'm sure you

don't need me to tell you what a wonderful specimen of manhood you are. And only a rutabaga could avoid feeling some sort of attraction." She slid from underneath his restraining arm and added, "But I also find Ron quite attractive . . . I'm sure you'll agree he's a most handsome man."

"I'm afraid I don't happen to have a good eye for men," he said blackly.

"And to answer your earlier question, no, sex did not enter my mind upon entering this particular bedroom. I've always found the sight of any bed quite evocative. Don't you?"

She left him scowling and hopefully doubting—she'd been absolutely truthful when she'd told him that she found Ron quite attractive, as she did many models in magazines or stars on TV. She of course was *not* attracted to them or Ron as she was to Grady—but it would keep him guessing. She didn't like to think of Grady, who appeared an expert on seduction, ruminating over the knowledge that she found him extremely enticing. Not while they were unchaperoned in the house, and when her juices, on slow burn since her divorce, had been brought to the boiling point a few short hours ago.

She was in the hall when his words reached her from behind the closed bathroom door, muffled but audible.

"Working in a hospital must sure play havoc with your libido, then."

While fixing lunch, Pamela smiled as she remembered Grady's parting comment. Although he'd insisted he was hungry and wanted steak—for which he offered to pay—Pamela decided he was going to get a lighter lunch. She'd insisted on his taking a pain pill, as well as countless glasses of juice and water.

The last few hours had been punctuated by calls from Grady, who was not adapting well to enforced inactivity.

As she sliced some green peppers to add to the salad, she almost cut her finger off when another of his bellows reached her all the way in the kitchen.

"Pamela! The ice water's all gone."

Pamela breathed deeply and counted to fifty—ten was no longer enough—and wondered if there was already a Saint Pamela. At this rate, she ought to be nominated for canonization.

After washing the cherry tomatoes and adding them to the large salad, she endured another "Pamela! Pamela, come here!" before drying her hands and marching on toward the bedroom she'd begun to consider a battle zone.

Chapter 6

SHORTLY BEFORE REACHING HIM, she heard a tremendous thud and the sound of glass breaking.

She ran the rest of the way, and gasped at the sight of Grady on all fours—or rather two and a half, since his left leg was extended straight by virtue of the cast, and he was awkwardly trying to place weight on his left elbow, his sling looking ludicrous as it curled about his neck and chin.

Pamela rushed forward, worried that Grady had cut himself or further aggravated his injuries. But once she saw there was no blood or any additional broken bones, she couldn't check the chuckle that escaped her.

Grady turned to look at her, his brows contracting as water streaked his hair and face in icy rivulets.

"I thought the ice water was gone," Pamela said with a straight face.

"It is now," Grady told her, his brows contracting even further. "I figured that worried as you are about me dehydrating, you would come running when I told you my supply was dimished."

"I was finishing the salad," she told him as she knelt next to him.

Grady's gaze glittered as he took in her flushed cheeks and dancing eyes, which could not entirely hide her amusement. He raised his hand, obviously with the intention of brushing the wet hair out of his eyes, but had to lower his hand immediately, or risk falling flat on his face.

"Could you help me to the bathroom again? It seems all this *liquid* has had a deleterious effect on me." Grady emphasized the word liquid, and Pamela smiled sunnily at him.

"Certainly. You need only ask."

Grady's look revealed a thunderstorm, and Pamela had him lean on her as she tried to lift his monolithic frame. "You know, I was considering taking weight-lifting classes. I think I'm getting a good start."

He grunted, and Pamela mentioned casually as they began another trek to the bathroom, "By the way, I'd like to change the dressing on your wrist—it's wet. When you're through, yell for me. You've had enough practice."

Grady let her get to the door before calling out.

"Pamela?"

She turned warily. "Yes?"

"I hurt my right hand when I fell off the bed. Can you get my briefs down?"

Pamela had managed to keep her eyes above his waistline, but at his words they automatically lowered to his loins. She cursed him silently for always emphasizing the difference the French celebrated, because since meeting him, *vive la différence* had become her body's anthem. She was having enough trouble trying to keep in mind that Grady was just her patient. She wondered how Alice managed; it must be the very devil for both patient and nurse to have to act professional when the forces of combustible chemistry were at work. And in her case, she was having enough trouble with visual gravity's pull without Grady calling attention to his considerable manly charms.

She resolved to talk to Alice soon about this sticky situation. In the meantime, she would have to wing it.

"I'm sure you can manage . . ."

"I could if I wore boxer shorts. But as you can see, these briefs tend to be rather restrictive."

When Pamela hesitated, feeling sensual heat flood her body and dissipate her hard-earned coolness, he added, "Of course, I could always skip the briefs and go nude. I'm sure the male anatomy holds no secrets for you."

It wasn't generic male anatomy that was concerning Pamela at this moment; it was Grady's specific, sexy one, and her own very female, very primal response to it.

Bracing herself, she pasted a professional smile on her face and told herself these next four days would pass.

She walked toward him calmly, resolving not to let on how disturbed she was. She reached him and looked downward just once, memorizing the relative position of his silver bikini briefs, and then stared straight ahead at the attractive hollow beneath his throat, where a few golden hairs clung like soft silk.

Grady, perverse being that he was, chose that moment to step back and say, "Would you hurry? I'm getting cramps."

Pamela gritted her teeth and extended her hands, but since Grady had shifted, her distance perception was affected, and her hands encountered a solid ridge of flesh, which moved and throbbed under her tentative touch.

Grady started, and he leaned down, whispering in her ear, "Want to play around?"

Pamela lifted her head, feeling her cheeks burn and her temper singe.

"No, I don't want to play around! I just want to get you better so you can leave and stop torturing me!"

His right hand miraculously recovered and she found herself pressed against his chest, their combined balance somewhat off as they teetered in the doorway.

"And how am I torturing you? I haven't even kissed you yet. Or is that the problem? Should I be less of a gentleman?"

"You wouldn't know a gentleman if one bit you in the rear!" Pamela exclaimed, beyond all patience.

She pushed against him with a mighty shove and grabbed hold of his briefs. With a violent motion, she ripped them from his narrow hips and flung the remnants at him.

"Here are your briefs! Now you can walk as naked as Adam if you wish, but I've had it. And you can also take care of your own needs as of right now!"

As she stormed out of the room, she heard his words, uttered in a sexy, amused tone. "Why, Pamela! I knew you were a passionate woman, but you exceed my wildest expectations. Should I get dressed so you can rip off all my clothes and satisfy your fiery soul?"

Pamela ate her light lunch in simmering fury, demolishing the salad with her small, even teeth in ferocious bites. The soup fared no better, and she found the crunch of the crackers infinitely satisfying in her ears.

But the silence bothered her. Grady had not called out to her again, and although not more than half an hour had elapsed, she began worrying that something might have happened. What if he had slipped and hit his forehead on the sink? What if he were unconscious at this very instant? Pamela could not forgive herself if he had come to harm.

Of course, he could be lying low, counting on her

conscience to be uneasy. He had seemed to penetrate her defenses like no other man had, realizing that she could not stand to see suffering or pain, and that she always felt compelled to help.

The hell with becoming involved, she told herself as she munched on a crisp apple. Why should she always be the softhearted dummy, an easy mark for anyone? Let him take care of himself. He was impossible.

But when another ten minutes went by and there was still no sound from Grady, she began to worry in earnest. Tiptoeing to his room, she paused outside the door and stealthily peeped in.

Obviously, Grady had been lying in wait. "Ah, there you are. Come to check if I've lived or died? Knew you wouldn't desert me. Lunch ready?"

Pamela straightened, feeling utterly ridiculous, sneaking around in her own house.

"Yes, lunch is ready," she told him with not a trace of friendliness. "You can come and get it."

"And risk another injury? If we don't do it right the first time, you might find me on your hands for an even longer time."

"Heaven forbid!" Pamela muttered.

As she began to head out to the kitchen again, Grady called uncertainly, "Pamela? I truly am starving."

"Really?"

"Can you help me into the kitchen?"

She retraced her steps and looked at him from the door with a sweet smile on her face. "But we wouldn't want you to overexert yourself, would we? And besides, I can't have you naked in the kitchen, can I? What if a neighbor drops by?"

"There are no neigh—I mean, I could just put on another pair of briefs. Or even my pajamas."

"Your hand's improved miraculously? It must be your prayers."

Grady grinned. "You could help me . . ." At her thundering expression, he quickly said, "All right, all right. Get me my pajama bottoms, and I'll put them on myself."

Pamela nodded and left, noting the pleased expression on his face.

When she returned, however, his pleased expression evaporated.

She was bringing his pajamas, all right . . . on one corner of the large tray bearing a huge bowl of salad and one of soup.

As she arranged the tray on his lap, he sighed and cupped her chin with his right hand. "How about your keeping me company while I eat? I'm going out of my skull with boredom."

Pamela looked about the room, and said, "You're right. You do need some entertainment. I've been remiss."

She left again and returned a few minutes later, finding he'd already finished the soup. The poor man must have been as ravenous as he'd said. With his bearlike constitution, he probably needed a constant replenishing of caloric fuel.

She set the small portable TV on the dresser and plugged it in. Then she took the magazines she'd piled on top of the television set and walked over to the bed, plopping them down next to him.

"There. That should keep you amused. And you mentioned you had a lot of paperwork to catch up on. I'll leave you to it."

As she turned to leave, she saw Grady's expression turn from one of flabbergasted surprise to disgust. She figured this battle was hers.

But there was still the war to be reckoned with.

Chapter 7

THE NEXT TWO days were a repeat of the first, an ebb and flow in Grady's temperature, as well as in his temper. Pamela knew how much he hated to be confined, so she tried to hold the reins on her own temper.

Saturday night she helped Grady into the dining room. His fever had disappeared, and both his wrist and shoulder were much improved. As she served the steak and baked potatoes he'd been badgering her for, Grady dropped another bombshell.

"Would you mind if I stayed on another week? I've gotten behind in my work and would appreciate having the extra time to recuperate and do some business over the phone." As Pamela opened her mouth to protest, he added, "I would, of course, pay you for my stay. The going rate at a motel, plus food and the phone bill."

Pamela shook her head. "It's not the money. I just can't take any more time off."

"I understand. But I'm an early riser. I could get up and have breakfast with you and dinner when you get home. Plus you'd be here to make sure no complications set in."

Sighing, Pamela met his gaze and said, "Okay. But my son's supposed to be back next weekend. My in-laws are driving him down, and you'll have to be out for sure by then. Eric is at the stage where he considers himself my protector and he would not appreciate seeing you on the premises."

"No problem," Grady assured her. "I'll leave Friday evening."

"What I don't understand is why you don't leave now," Pamela said, puzzled. "What kind of business did you say you were in?"

"All kinds. Right now I'm sort of a promoter. I've always liked sports, and plan to get more involved in that."

That was still very cleverly vague. She wanted to question Grady further, but he began complimenting her on dinner.

"This is ambrosia," he enthused. "What's for dessert?"

Pamela couldn't help laughing. "Cherry pie. That was one of the favorites you included on your list of epicurean delights."

His eye shone. "Great! I'm a pretty good cook myself, and I'll return the favor when I'm back to normal."

"You mean being a steamroller and con artist does not come naturally to you?" Pamela asked as she finished her potatoes. "And about that list you made . . ."

"Took hours of painstaking work. I'm practically useless with my right hand."

As she began to stack the dishes, Pamela looked at him skeptically, but she really couldn't take him to task on that one. *She* was totally useless with her left hand, so perhaps he was telling the truth.

She took the loaded tray into the kitchen, and when

she came back with dessert, Grady asked, "Are you any good at typing?"

"I have a self-correcting machine. Actually, it's Eric's, but he's using Helena's while he's in Illinois. If you don't require speed, I suppose I can help you."

"You're a real trooper, Pamela Shaw. I appreciate your volunteering." The way his eyes caressed her buxom figure told her that wasn't all he appreciated.

The following morning Pamela allowed Grady to go outside. The day was mild and sunny, and he sat on a garden lounger, propping his leg and arm on pillows Pamela brought out for him.

She fixed a folding table and chair for herself in the back porch, and proceeded to type out letters for Grady on the heavy bond stationery he'd requested she buy.

They worked for three hours without interruption. As Grady dictated correspondence going to all four corners of the globe, Pamela realized that his company was quite diversified, with oil, shipping, and real-estate interests.

Abruptly, he stopped and looked out at the lake. His eyes took on a faraway expression and there was a cast of sadness to his features.

Softly, afraid of intruding but unable to stand the hurt on his face, Pamela asked, "Thinking about your wife?"

Grady returned to earth, his unseeing gaze shifting from the lake that sparkled like an aquamarine gem amid gray-yellow bluffs and emerald foliage.

He nodded. "It's been two years, but I still miss her. She was a marine biologist."

"And water reminds you of her," Pamela supplied gently as his voice cracked.

She could see his eyes had teared, and he didn't seem afraid to show emotion. Pamela felt her own eyes filling in empathy, and she hurriedly blinked. Unlike Grady, Pamela was scared to show her vulnerability.

"Laurel was a beautiful woman. Inside and out. And

the boys still miss her greatly. They idolized her."

Pamela felt as if there had been a faint warning in his words. But how could there be? She'd never meet his boys. Once he was mobile, he'd return to Ohio. And she'd never see him again.

Grady took a deep breath of the sweet-smelling air, already potent from the fragrance of early summer flowers, and Pamela watched the deep chest expand within the confines of the cream knit shirt. She remembered overhearing some of his telephone conversations with his boys. During one in particular, Grady had raised his voice considerably in reply to what Adam had said on the other end. It must have been hard on the boys, losing their mother . . .

"It's been difficult trying to relieve the boys' sense of loss, and anger and pain and frustration. It was not so bad with Damien and Benji. Damien was only four when we lost Laurel, and Benji has always been a realistic, very independent kid. But Adam and Craig really took it hard. Adam, as the first born, was especially close to Laurel. And Craig has always been a sensitive boy. He had wanted to be an oceanographer, and couldn't wait for the summer vacations, when we always headed out to some island, or lake, or the ocean. After Laurel died, the bottom dropped out for him—he withdrew, became sullen, lost all interest in the sea and anything dealing with marine life."

"Is he—is he all right now?" Pamela asked, uncertain as to how much she should probe, or how much he wanted to reveal at this memory-filled moment.

"He's fine, now, yes. But both Adam and Craig scrutinize every woman they see me with—not that there have been that many, outside of those I work with. But even my female colleagues come under heavy suspicion."

"They're not ready to let go of their mother's memory," Pamela ventured softly. "She must have been a wonderful woman."

Grady met her eyes and she almost drowned in his cloud-gray gaze. "She was. Like you. But there comes a time when we must let go. And I guess I was just saying good-bye to Laurel."

Pamela panicked. She found it hard to breathe, felt trapped by the gray eyes that seemed to be pinning her down.

She was not ready.

"I—ah—I think I better start lunch," she said, getting up precipitously and almost overturning the typewriter from its wobbly perch.

"Pamela!"

She didn't turn around, but told him as she hurried into the house, "I'll bring it out to the porch when it's ready."

The rest of the day passed uneventfully. Pamela knew Grady wanted to continue the conversation she'd so abruptly ended at lunchtime. But she didn't give him a chance.

It was no longer a question of his being a patient. Obviously, Grady aspired to being much more, and Pamela did not want to deal with that kind of involvement just yet. Her body might be craving a physical relationship, but her mind urged caution. She had just made a courageous move gambling on a new job, taking on the responsibility for a new house. There was still Eric to raise, and his feelings to consider.

And Pamela needed to sort out her own emotions. Grady might be a handsome, charming man, and there had been instant attraction between the two of them. But he also lived in another state. And he had four boys of his own. She had to be careful not to let her physical needs after a few years abstinence overwhelm her common sense, cloud her judgment. Too many things were at stake.

Grady might have said good-bye to his past, but Pamela didn't feel totally free to embark on a complicated, emotionally perilous future with him.

Pamela returned to work on Monday, but skipped lunch so she could be home sooner. Grady made steady progress, and by Wednesday was well enough to offer his help in putting up the hammock a friend had picked up for Pamela in Mexico last year.

"Are you certain you can manage?" Pamela asked doubtfully.

"Sure. I can use my right hand, and you don't need finesse so much as muscle right now. Where do you want it?"

Pamela suggested putting it in the back porch, but Grady told her it was already crowded with the patio furniture.

"How about between those two trees? It's near the lake, and surrounded by all those flowers. The ideal spot."

Pamela could see the merits of the suggestion, but asked, "What about when it rains? The vendor assured my friend this hammock is made wide enough so that it won't easily overturn, or turn one into a human salami. But I'm afraid the colors will fade if soaked too often and then dried by the sun, and also the material might rot sooner."

"So you bring it in when it rains. I'll make a special knot so that it will be easy to put up and take down again."

Grady showed her how to make the knot, and Pamela saw that indeed he did have problems with mobility and efficiency in his right hand. He managed to tie the knot the first time with Pamela's help, and then he helped her put up the huge, Aztec-designed hammock, while she secured the two ends to the trees.

"There. You did a good job."

Pamela smiled, liking the effect of the colorful hammock against the more placid blue of the lake. Its vivid hues—purple, green, red, orange, rust, royal blue—seemed to blend in with the refreshing, renewing colors of summer.

"Can I try it out?" Grady asked.

Pamela hesitated. "I don't know. It might not be—"

"Safe?" Grady supplied, standing braced against one of the tall trees. "What do you fear the most . . . my lack of expertise in nautical tying of knots, or the fact that I might be too heavy for your hammock?"

Put that way, Pamela didn't know how to answer. Grady was big but not fat. His body was composed of delicious-looking and well-choreographed muscle and sinew. But the combination of his weight and the possibility that the knot might slip and he could end up on the ground.

"I know. You're afraid I might injure myself and impose on your hospitality even longer." He read her mind with startling accuracy, but then, they'd been living in very close quarters, and had had long conversations on all kinds of subjects, from the very trivial to music and art, managing to stay away from very personal topics.

"Well . . . now that you mention it . . ."

"Will you take my word that the hammock will hold? I will not be doing any somersaults in the air."

His tone was solemn, but Pamela could see silver devils dancing in his eyes.

Her rapidly dissipating resistance to his forceful and engaging personality, and equally strong physical magnetism, was getting to be a drag. Pamela knew the effect Grady had on her, and knew he knew she knew. The result was a constant clash of wills, where neither was the clear victor but where Pamela had all the more to lose.

"Go ahead," she said none too graciously, resentful of his power over her. "You may as well try it out for me. I certainly can't afford to be laid up with broken bones for a week or two."

He ignored her pointed dig, and skipping the crutch, held on to the tree instead as he positioned himself next to the hammock. "Would you give me a hand? Hold the hammock still while I lower myself onto it?"

Pamela approached and helped maneuver Grady into a sitting position. She had to admit, this hammock was certainly an improvement on others she had seen, which were so unstable they resembled trampolines.

"See, it's holding," Grady said. "Can you help me lie down?"

She leaned forward, but he let himself fall back suddenly, and she found herself pitching forward, almost catapulting over the hammock but for Grady's strong-armed hold.

She raised her face from his armpit and regarded him with glittering hazel eyes. "Very clever. Now let me up."

"Oh, come on," he told her, his breath tickling her ear in a very pleasant fashion. "You have to relax for a while. You've been too uptight."

Resting her elbow on Grady's wide chest, she felt his body hardening beneath hers. Putting more of her body weight into her elbows, she said dreamily, "You know, you're absolutely right. I need to slow down, and this is not only a beautiful spot to relax in, but also a very comfortable one." She looked down at his slightly contorted features, and asked, "Are you comfy?"

"Oh, definitely," he groaned. He tried to move his chest away from her elbows, and Pamela could feel the muscles working beneath the tight, smooth skin that his denim vest laid bare. "Grady, watch out, we don't want to move, and all that. Remember?"

Her studiedly innocent expression gave her away, and Grady said, "Why, you little . . . I knew there had to be a reason for your sudden compliance." With his right arm, he swatted at her elbows, and caught her as her chest, covered by a sundress, met his with sudden abruptness. "Now I'm comfy," he told her with eminent satisfaction as the halter-type shirred bodice allowed a lot of her flesh to come into contact with his desire-moist skin.

"Well, I'm not," Pamela retorted, putting her palms on his bare, broad shoulders to push herself up and away from his disturbing body.

His shoulders bunched under her touch, and his biceps increased in reflex action. His eyes grew a dark gray, and his whole body underwent a total transformation, preparing him for love.

"Lord how I want you, Pamela." As she looked at him, mesmerized by the passion and need in him and by her own helpless, automatic response to his male urgency, Grady told her hoarsely, "And you can't deny that you want me."

Pamela opened her mouth to deny just that. The fact that it was true should not mean that she was going to admit it, or give in to it.

Grady cupped the back of her head with an unsteady hand, and told her, "I gave you my promise that I'd behave. That's why I'm warning you. I'm going to kiss you. If you want to stop me, you'll have to do it."

Pamela looked down at Grady, and when his long fingers extended to caress the sensitive skin at the base of her neck and at the sides, she whimpered.

"You're not being fair," she said, surprised at the thickness of her own voice.

"I never said I'd be fair. But it's your choice. You know where I stand."

His fingers began to untie the halter straps of her white sundress, while his left hand traced a hand-painted violet and its small cluster of emerald leaves at her waist.

When she didn't stop him, Grady lowered the thin straps and let them dangle on each side of her. Pamela tried to think, tried to reason, but all that emerged from the mélange in her mind was want, desire, a need to be close to a man. No, not to *a* man. To Grady.

She surrendered to that need.

As Grady raised his head to kiss her throat and the pulse throbbing there in racing rhythm with her runaway heartbeat, Pamela gave in to her long-held impulse to bury her fingers in his hair. The silken strands caressed her fingertips, and when Grady lowered his lips to the upper swell of her breast, her fingers tightened almost painfully in frenzied response.

She buried her mouth in his hair, inhaling the clean, lemony scent, and lowered a hand to trace his ear, circling it teasingly before invading the shell with an inquisitive, deliberate digit.

Grady's rough exhalation of breath blistered her fevered flesh, and he lifted his head from her heaving breasts to seek her mouth.

Pamela slid down on the hammock, careful of his leg as she settled between the pulsating valley where male leg joined hip, and she sought his lips with blind need.

But as their hungry mouths touched, and Grady's hold tightened convulsively on her, a scandalized, horrified high voice rent the air.

"Mother!"

Chapter 8

THE SINGLE WORD was a veritable ice bucket on Pamela's ardor. She stiffened against Grady's arm and moaned in maternal despair.

Grady had heard the short scream too, but he was slower in reacting: he hadn't recognized the adolescent voice as Pamela had. Fourteen-year-old Eric's voice change was almost complete, but his husky tenor failed him at critical times, particularly when he was over-excited.

"Mother? Are you all right?"

Eric's tone had shifted from accusation to fear. He obviously wanted very badly to believe that his mother had been forced into lovemaking. In a weak moment, Pamela almost wished she had. She dreaded meeting her son's blue gaze.

But she lifted the head she'd buried in Grady's shoulder in an instant of panic and mortification. Getting quickly to her feet, she faced her son squarely.

"Yes, Eric. I'm fine."

His shocked, disbelieving gaze went from Pamela to Grady and back again, taking in her flushed cheeks, bright eyes, and disheveled dress. Disgust and shame quickly followed in the wake of his other emotions, and Pamela was dismayed to read them in the expressive, youthful face.

"I came early because I was worried about you," Eric said bitterly. "I was afraid you'd be lonely." He pointed to the hammock with a gesture showing disgust and disappointment, and above all, hurt. "But I didn't have to worry, did I? You probably wish I'd stayed away longer, so you could . . . could . . ." Pamela could see her son's painful choosing and discarding of several verbs, until he finished, ". . . screw him without interruption."

He pivoted to go back into the house and Pamela closed her eyes as his words stabbed into her heart, causing the anguish only a child can administer so accurately and piercingly, even if wrongly and unfairly. She had missed her son but had wanted him to finish his school year and have some fun. Now, he'd sacrificed some parties to be with her, and Pamela could understand how Eric was feeling. Which made *her* feel guilty and miserable.

As Grady moved, obviously to go to her defense, Pamela stepped in front of him. She didn't want him to address her son and possibly trigger off a volley of insults.

"Eric, how did you get here?" she asked her son sharply.

Eric opened the door, and Pamela heard the hammock creak slightly as Grady got up. Not wanting to address her son's back, she spoke louder.

"Eric!"

The boy didn't turn around. Despite her feelings of guilt, Pamela would not tolerate rudeness and insubordination.

"Turn around and look at me." After a slight hesitation, Eric turned to face her with a sullen expression that Pamela knew hid a great deal of hurt and consternation. "How did you get here?" she asked him.

"What do you care? You've got your lover boy there—"

"Eric!"

Grady had hobbled to stand next to her, leaning on his crutch, and Eric's expression hardened into dislike and male challenge.

"Boy, I used to think my *father* was a skirt chaser, but I guess things stay in the family. Or maybe it's contagious. Now Mom's after anything in pants . . ."

Grady moved forward threateningly and spoke for the first time. "You'd better watch that mouth, boy. Apologize to—"

"Grady, please!" Pamela laid her hand on Grady's clenched fist to pacify him. "You still haven't answered my question, Eric."

Her son's blue gaze fell before her level hazel one and Eric muttered, "I came by bus."

"You took the bus? Why?"

"I told you! I wanted to surprise you. And boy, did I!"

Grady took another step, and Pamela moved forward with him, holding on to his good arm. Eric looked from one to the other and continued, "I wanted to come here sooner. I was worried about you. And I figured I'd save Uncle Barrett and Aunt Helena a trip. They're both real busy at work. Anyway, it was a fun trip, neat scenery."

"And how did you get here from the bus station?" Pamela's voice had acquired a dangerous edge; she had a pretty good idea of what her son had done.

Eric shuffled from one foot to the other. He kept his gaze down and his hands in the pockets of his grimy, well-worn Levis.

"Eric, I asked you a question."

"I hitchhiked," he mumbled.

"You what!"

"You heard me. And anyway, what's the big deal?" Eric's tone turned defiant again. He probably thought he had a good whip to lash Pamela with. "Would you even have noticed if I'd disappeared, or if anything had happened to me? The moment my back is turned..."

If Pamela hadn't felt so much like screaming, she'd have laughed at her son's pseudo-adult tone and language. She could feel Grady go rigid next to her. She knew he was suppressing what he wanted to say out of deference to her, and she appreciated the tremendous effort. She'd have to deal with this one alone, and Grady was not aware of Eric's special circumstances, or his earlier vulnerability.

"Eric. Go into the house and put the spaghetti water on to boil. I'll be in shortly."

"Is he eating here too? Because if he is, I'm not hungry."

"I don't care what you are, Eric. I had planned spaghetti for this weekend, because it's one of your favorite meals. Since you came early, you can have it tonight."

Pamela knew she was pushing it. She was treating him like a child in front of another male—a natural rival at that. And Eric was already more than halfway to being a man himself.

But she had to assert her authority. Eric might be her first priority, her first love, but he had to understand she was a woman, too. She would discuss that later. Right now he had to see that she was still his mother, responsible for his welfare, and no matter what happened, who intervened, he would always be her son.

Rebellion flared in the beautiful blue eyes. But Pamela stared him down, and the mother in her won.

Eric turned and slammed into the house.

Grady stepped in front of her and cupped her chin. "You know you can't let it go at that. You have nothing to be ashamed of."

"I know, but reason and feeling are two different things. I also know what's going on in my son's head and am painfully aware this has been quite a shock to him."

"I gather Trevor was not the faithful type."

Pamela shook her head. She tied the halter straps in back of her neck and told him, "No. I gave him a second chance, but it barely lasted a year. I've been divorced for almost three years, and Eric has never seen me with another man."

Grady caressed her cheek when a lonely tear that Pamela hadn't been able to contain splashed onto it.

"You can't do that to yourself, Pamela. You can't make up for your husband's infidelity. You have your own needs, and the right to fulfill them."

"Right now, those needs seem insignificant next to Eric's hurt and sense of betrayal." She squeezed Grady's hand in gratitude, but lowered it from her face. "I have to go in and talk to him, Grady. Alone."

He nodded and awkwardly straightened her shirred bodice, which had lowered to expose most of the upper curve of her breast.

"I'm sorry. I didn't mean to cause you this kind of problem, or a rift between you and your son." He smiled ruefully. "I'd hoped he'd like me, but I couldn't have gotten off to a worse start." Leaning on his crutch, he started toward the house. "I'll get my things and call a taxi."

Pamela detained him. "No you don't. You were going to stay until this weekend. I won't have you chased off by my son as if we were guilty."

Grady's right hand came up to caress her inner elbow, causing chills to chase up her arm and diffuse into her spine. "You think that's wise? It's going to be highly volatile around here."

"I know. But you're the first man I've kissed since the divorce." At his raised brows, she laughed, feeling better at the slight release of tension. "Tried to kiss," she amended, "and I'm not going to wear sackcloth or a T-shirt with a scarlet A on it. Eric has to come around."

Grady looked at her for long moment, and Pamela's senses perked up again, resuming the heightened level they'd attained while she was on the hammock. If Grady could do this with a hot look or a slight caress, what could he do to her while making love? A long, sensual shudder shook her at the thought.

Grady smiled, reading her response, and told her, "I'd better watch myself around your son. But it's not going to be easy if I have to go around in a state of perpetual frustration."

"You've got two choices," Pamela told him, standing on tiptoe to kiss his clean-shaven cheek. Grady had managed to shave with a minimum of cuts using his right hand, but he'd deferred without demur when Pamela had offered to do it for him. "You can either take very cold showers, or I'll drive you to an appropriate part of town to satisfy your cravings."

His arm came up to pull her against him, but Pamela nimbly evaded him.

"Only you can satisfy this fire, Pamela. And I hope you can take me out of my misery soon."

Pamela laughed as she ran up the porch steps. "One male problem at a time, please. And remember, no promises of any kind."

Grady followed at a slower pace, his crutch hitting the ground in released frustration. "For someone in the medical field, Pamela," he called to her quickly retreating figure, "you're showing very little compassion lately."

"Mom, what's this ugly bird doing in the kitchen?"

Pamela laughed at the affront in Eric's voice. She'd gone upstairs to put her hair up and change into a canary-yellow jumpsuit. It was soft and loose and comfortable, with long dolman sleeves and a modest neck.

"That's J.L., Eric. He had an accident and I've been fixing him up."

"Just like you're fixing Mr. Macho outside?"

Pamela looked at the back of Eric's head, tilted proudly and aggressively, and sighed. All right then—if he wanted to have it out now, she wouldn't duck the issue.

Walking toward where her son stood by the sink, she leaned against the cold lime enamel and said, "Okay, Eric. You're itching for a confrontation. And while I'm not going to oblige you, I *will* answer your questions and then we will shelve the subject. Agreed?"

Eric stared straight ahead, but Pamela was sure he was not taking in the view of the sun-bathed lake out the kitchen window.

She repeated, "Agreed? No more discussions, no more accusations, after this?"

Eric finally looked at her and Pamela could see the little boy in the hurt blue eyes, eyes that Trevor's betrayal, not only of her, but especially of his son's trust and worshipful adoration, had made mature beyond their years.

Wanting to erase the bewilderment and confusion in the young-old eyes, Pamela found she began to blame herself again. She had to forcibly remind herself she'd tried to give Eric all the love she could—except for that very black period in her life when she'd been so afraid of losing her husband she'd neglected her own son. But she had pulled herself together, making a new life for herself and Eric. Then she had given Trevor another chance, but Trevor's promises didn't signify much. Now, Pamela felt she was transported back in time four years before Eric's accusing look: Only this time, Eric's sense of betrayal stemmed from her own actions.

Breathing deep, calming breaths, trying to still the trembling that invaded her body and reminded her of the old Pamela, afraid and insecure, she asked evenly, "What is it you're mad at? Or hurt by? Or disgusted with? Talk to me."

Eric's gaze dropped before hers, and Pamela almost smiled. She knew her son was feeling self-conscious; she'd tried to talk to him about sex, but he'd told her he'd rather discuss it further with his uncle Barrett. Not without some relief, Pamela had agreed.

But now things were at too critical a stage to let mutual discomfort interfere.

"Is it the thought of your mother having sex with a man? I know sometimes children find it hard to think of their parents as sexual beings . . ."

"No!" Pamela started at his forceful denial and Eric fidgeted, met her gaze, then looked down at his hands, which were playing with the mushroom-shaped salt shaker.

"I guess that's part of it too," he admitted in a low voice. "But it's more than that."

"Do you think I should go on forever without a relationship with a man? Women have needs, too, Eric—even mothers. For me it's been over three years . . ."

"I know! I know! I learned about all that in class . . ."

Pamela let that pass. "Then what? Why did you act so affronted and disgusted? I know it was a surprise to you—maybe something of a shock. But believe me, we were no less startled." Humor crept into her tone at the understatement; she'd felt on the verge of a heart attack and Grady's groan had testified to his own dismay and certain discomfort, both mental and physical.

When Eric didn't answer, she continued softly, "Sex is not dirty, Eric. It can be the most beautiful, delicate expression—"

"How long have you known this man, Mother?"

Eric looked her straight in the eye and Pamela answered, "A few days. I—"

"Don't you think he could be taking advantage of you? Men are different from women, Mom. All they want is sex . . ."

Pamela was touched by the concern in her son's tone. But she didn't want him to remain with a misconception.

"When you grow up—" At his offended expression, she substituted quickly, "when you're a bit older, you'll see men and women are not all that different. Sex can be very important to women, and men need love, too."

"Yes, but you can get hurt. He could be just like Dad . . ."

Pamela put her hands in the wide pockets of her jumpsuit and dug her nails into her palms. Trevor had done so much damage that even these last four years of stability and warmth and affection had not erased all Eric's pain and insecurity.

"Your father's not perfect, Eric, but he's trying the best way he knows how. He'll never be faithful to any one woman, and that's the way he is. But he did love me and he's learning to love you. He's not as strong as your uncles, and you have to help him get over his own insecurities."

Eric's expression changed and Pamela could see he was giving some thought to this. He'd never looked at his father in this light, and she hoped this new angle would help Eric deal with his own demons and prevent him from judging his father too harshly.

"Whenever you feel like blaming your father, Eric, remember, he's human."

Eric met her gaze and she could read shame and contrition alongside the remaining doubts.

"I guess I acted like a jerk . . ." he began uncertainly.

Pamela raised her hand and ruffled his hair. She'd been yearning to touch her son, to hug him and kiss him with the sheer joy of having him back.

Eric's arms lifted slightly, awkwardly, and Pamela interpreted the uncertain gesture correctly. She removed the foot separating them and hugged him, surprised anew at how much he'd grown in a few weeks. Eric had been taller than she for the past year already, and he was going to be as tall as his father and uncle.

"I missed you, Eric. I'm glad you came home early. I wanted you to have fun, but I'm real happy and proud that you skipped those parties to join me here."

"Aw, they weren't that great," Eric said, embarrassed, and tried to pull out of the embrace. But Pamela held on to his arms as he asked, "Are you sure you want me around? I might put a damper on things, so I could just go back to Illinois for a while . . ."

"Eric Shaw, hear this. Even if I were having the most wonderful sex with the sexiest man in the world every night—and day—I would want you here. You're my son and I love you. And no matter that I'm a woman and have my needs and am quite normal and like men: I'm your mother and will always love you. Got that?"

Eric had turned beet red and was trying to squiggle out of her grasp. "Yeah, I hear you," he said, his ears burning and his tone mortified. Pamela let go of her son, but not before planting a big smacking kiss on his cheek and chin.

"Aw, Mom," Eric protested, his hand automatically lifting to rub away the kisses as he'd done when he was a child. He stopped in time, flustered, and Pamela gave him a quick hug, laughing.

"I have to take advantage of the moment, Eric," she told him at his less-than-pleased expression. Her son wanted to feel loved and secure, but at a distance.

"You know, it's not easy on the mother, either. As children grow up, they start developing their own lives, and begin separating from their parents. Which is as it should be. But no matter how much a mother tries to let go, it's not easy." She smiled as Eric grimaced, knowing he'd had enough of this heart-to-heart, now that he'd been reassured.

"I know, Mom," Eric said, and began backing out of the kitchen.

"Hey, take J.L. outside. He can use the fresh air."

Rumbling under his breath, Eric took the box and eyed the sea gull distastefully. His preferences ran more toward German shepherds, boa constrictors, and lizards.

Pamela went to the refrigerator to take out the makings

for a salad and dessert, but her son's voice caused her to turn around.

"Mom, I'm sorry I acted like such a nerd. I promise to be—to be, ah . . . polite, to your . . . guest."

Pamela's eyes filled with tears, and she felt like hugging her son again. She ignored the cautiousness of the promise, and the dubious categorizing of Grady. The apology was very handsome, and she knew how hard it had been for Eric to make it.

Although her heart swelled with tenderness and pride, she contented herself with saying merely, "That'd be real nice, Eric."

Dinner was a rather strained affair. Even though Eric did keep his promise and was polite to Grady, he tried to take a few potshots at his mother's friend. Grady fielded Eric's sallies gracefully and peacefully. Although both Grady and Pamela tried to draw Eric into the conversation, beyond those digging forays, the boy confined his answers to monosyllables.

At one point, after telling his mother to remain seated and getting the strawberry shortcake from the kitchen, he asked about J.L. Pamela, happy her son was contributing more than a single word, went on to explain the circumstances regarding both J.L.'s accident, and Grady's injuries and his subsequent stay.

"Do you intend to keep the sea gull for long?"

Pamela laughed. "Come on, Eric, I know you haven't particularly liked birds as pets ever since your parakeets refused to talk and the cockatiel your father gave you almost took off your finger and nose. But you must admit, J.L. is rather pitiful."

"I thought Mad Max was rather pitiful too, but I've got the scar to prove otherwise." While Grady looked on amused as Eric showed a finger where a tiny scar remained, Pamela quickly narrated the harrowing experience.

"His uncle gave him a pair of parakeets, which Eric named Adam and Eve—"

"Yeah, and they were too busy cooing to do much talking, except when they were hungry. They sure learned, 'Feed me, feed me,' quick enough," Eric put in morosely.

"We couldn't have pets in the condominium where we lived, so for his tenth birthday Eric got a beautiful big aquarium from Helena, and the parakeets from Barrett."

"And one of the neighbors' cats ate up most of my fish," Eric put in.

"I thought you couldn't have pets," Grady asked, puzzled, as he accepted another serving of dessert.

"We couldn't, but most people sneaked in something."

"I almost got that Alleycat, too," Eric said, his face screwed in vengeful remembrance.

"Alleycat?"

"That was Eric's nickname for the cat," Pamela told Grady. "His owner, a sweet old lady living a few doors down, had named him Marshmallow."

"And I sure would have liked to roast him," Eric told Grady, adding with manly indulgence, "But Mom wouldn't let me. She told me the cat was too pretty to stick in the oven, and besides, it was doing what comes naturally to cats."

Grady choked on some homemade whipped cream and said, "I suspect your mother was right. And she was probably also worried about the sweet old lady's feelings, too, and any possible repercussions for you should you have demanded an eye for an eye."

"Yeah, well, Mrs. Johnson was real nice—she always made cookies and she even brought cut fruit and raw potatoes for Mad Max."

"We had to eventually give him away," Pamela explained. "Trevor bought him the cockatiel for his eleventh birthday, since the parakeets were not working out . . ."

"But Dad's present was even worse," Eric put in.

"I must admit, Mad Max was aptly named. He was

a feathered version of a vicious psychotic, and he even had suicidal tendencies."

"I don't think so," Eric said as he served himself more shortcake for the third time. He caught Pamela's eye and smiled, knowing that he usually would not get away with that, but he was milking his homecoming for all it was worth. Pamela shook her head in smiling remonstrance, but didn't say anything, her son's rascally grin tugging at her heartstrings. As he had known it would, the little con artist.

"Eric still maintains the bird became violent each time he saw him . . ."

"Yeah. Didn't you see how he used to lunge at the cage, shaking it and trying to demolish the bars." As he swiftly disposed of his dessert, Eric added dolefully, "I just haven't had that much luck with pets. And all I wanted was a large, very large dog. Which we could never have while we lived in Courtland Square."

This last was said directly at Pamela, who calmly stared back. With more emphasis, Eric said, "Of course, we no longer live in a condo . . ."

"Quite an astute observation," Pamela said, grinning. She knew her son wanted a dog, and she intended to get him one. But right now, there was something else that had not been discussed yet. "Eric, about your ride here this afternoon . . ."

"Uh, Mom, may I be excused? I am kind of tired after the trip."

Pamela's gaze met Grady's across the table, and Eric intercepted it.

Eric asked with some challenge in his voice, "You're not thinking of keeping the sea gull, are you?"

"No, of course not. You know how I feel about wild creatures. He should be able to fly away in a few days."

"And Mr. Talliver. How long does he have yet?"

Well, the truce was over. Pamela sighed, having enjoyed the little peaceful interlude, and said, "Grady will be leaving this weekend. As I was responsible for incapacitating him, and Grady's left-handed, I agreed to help him out for a few days."

Eric's relief was obvious, but he had one last question as he got up and laid his napkin on the table. "And he couldn't find a private nurse?"

Eric's suspicious glance went from Grady to her, and she answered calmly, "You know this part of Michigan is pretty isolated, Eric. He couldn't have found someone right away, and I didn't mind doing it." As Grady's thick brows lifted, she added, "Much," and took a sip of wine to hide her wry smile.

Eric watched the byplay and frowned. "I can type, and I took some accounting in school, Mr. Talliver. I can help you, too."

The unspoken, "So you can leave as soon as possible," vibrated in the air, but Grady answered the boy with quiet gratitude. "I'd really appreciate that, Eric."

Pamela could tell Eric was a bit shamefaced, but he quickly hid it beneath his tough-guy mask and said, "Good night."

"Good night, Eric. I'll be up to talk to you in a little while," she told him.

Eric looked puzzled for a moment and then his tough mask slipped as comprehension dawned on him, and was joined by a little healthy apprehension. He nodded and left the room in his lanky gait, his body not having caught up with his long arms and legs.

Pamela and Grady watched him leave, and Grady said, "Your son has a rotten sense of timing, but I must say he can't be faulted on his protectiveness. He watches me like a hawk, and now it's going to be even harder to make a move."

"I thought you'd already made a move," Pamela said as she got up to clear the table.

"An aborted one. And I've got the feeling it's going to be crowded around here."

Pamela laughed and Grady got up awkwardly, helping her to stack some dishes.

"You were lucky to have my undivided attention so long," Pamela told him. "But my son is a vital part of my life."

She realized that *she* was now giving Grady a warning. Pamela wanted Grady to know how important Eric was to her.

Grady leaned on his crutch, and Pamela realized that the time they'd spent outside had exhausted him. His face was lined with pain and his skin was somewhat pale underneath its bronze casting. But he would sleep well tonight.

"You're forgetting I have four of my own," he reminded her gently. "Don't worry, I'm quite aware of how Eric's feeling. Plus I've been put through the wringer before, and have seen my few dates go through regular inquisitions."

Pamela smiled and dropped a kiss on the rough cheek, where blond stubble was beginning to show. She was grateful for his understanding and wry humor and communicated her appreciation with that kiss. The smile Grady flashed her in return thanked her for the gesture . . . but at the same time let her know he wanted a very different kind of kiss from her.

All in good time, Pamela telegraphed him with her eyes. All in good time.

Chapter 9

A HALF-HOUR LATER, Pamela went up to Eric's room and asked him how he liked it now that she'd had it repainted in his choice, sky-blue.

Eric answered, "Fine, Mom. And I know what's coming. I shouldn't have hitchhiked. I should have taken a taxi."

"Well, that's one way of taking the sails out of a parent's lecture," Pamela said, sitting on the bed covered by a navy-and-gray-striped bedspread. "But you're not out of the woods yet. You might think you're mature and strong, Eric, but you're still quite young and vulnerable. Things happen to boys, too, not only to girls. Next time you feel indestructible and want to take chances, just think how I'd feel if you suddenly disappeared, or were kidnapped."

Eric straightened from his lazy sprawl and said soberly, "I will. Some homecoming this has turned out to be."

Pamela looked at his glum face and saw the child lurking there. Deciding he'd had enough scolding and severity for one day, she got up and asked, "Have you inspected your room yet?"

Eric looked around and shrugged his shoulders. "Not yet. I saw the room when we were here before, looking over the property. It's nice, but a room's a room."

Pamela smiled. Opening the closet, she got out a black case. "Well, there is something new in this room I thought you'd like."

Eric bounded out of bed and Pamela handed him the case. "Happy homecoming."

Opening the case, Eric took out the gleaming instrument. "A brand new sax." He ran his hands reverently over the smooth golden surface. "Thanks, Mom."

He dropped a quick kiss on her cheek and asked eagerly, "Do you think I can practice a bit? There's a music book in here."

Grinning, Pamela said, "I thought you were tired."

Eric grinned back. "I can handle half an hour of practice before passing out."

Pamela's eyes gleamed. "I don't think Grady's going to cope too well with the noise."

Some of the joy left Eric's face. "You don't want me to disturb him?" he asked flatly.

"Oh, by all means, do. Grady told me he has four sons, so noise should not be foreign to him." As she saw the sudden, intense glee in her son's eyes, Pamela worried about having given him permission. Eric's practicing on guitar and sax were always enthusiastic, but she had the feeling this one was going to be special.

She blew Eric a kiss as he began to set up his instrument, checking out the reed and mouthpiece, and adjusting the neck strap to his long torso. He nodded to her as he began to spit into his mouthpiece, and Pamela had an unaccustomed fit of giggles as she anticipated Grady's reaction.

She didn't have to wait long. As the first loud, discordant notes filled the air, Pamela heard an equally loud groan emerging from the guest room.

An hour later, a fluid, mellifluous "Wreck of the John B" was replaced by an ear-breaking "Caissons Go Rolling Along." Pamela put the pillow over her head, but the blasting vibrations seemed to permeate her very bones. And there was no escaping the lethal music: All three bedrooms were on the second floor.

Suddenly, her door burst open, and Grady stood silhouetted against the door by the light of her bedside lamp, his upper torso a symphony of beautifully synchronized bronzed musculature, his hair golden in the soft illumination.

His scowling expression soon plucked Pamela from her romantic—as well as visceral—appreciation of the masculine symmetry leaning on a crutch, and she asked in dulcet tones, "Anything the matter?"

"Anything the matter?" Grady repeated incredulously. "Aren't your eardrums affected by that racket?" He moved into the room and asked suspiciously, "Or do you have ear plugs on?"

Pamela moved her head to show him pink, empty ears, and said, unable to keep maternal pride out of her voice, "Don't you think Eric plays rather well?"

As he hobbled closer, Grady muttered, "I wouldn't know. My hearing's been permanently impaired. I knew that kid disliked me, but this is torture of the highest degree. And you're an accomplice, allowing him to—"

As he stood by the bed, his voice died. His glance took in her sheer silver chiffon night gown, and the hair that, released once more from its confinement, covered one side of her face and reached her shoulders in a golden-brown cloud.

He attempted to speak, cleared his throat, tried again, and gave up altogether.

As if hypnotized, his gray eyes roamed her ivory shoulders and well-turned arms, her graceful neck and the twin mounds thrusting pertly above the black and silver-leafed sheet. Then his gaze met hers again and he leaned forward, balancing on one crutch and the hand that he put on the carved headboard of her bed.

Pamela felt her blood rush in her veins. Her ears shut out all extraneous noise, her body attuned only to the look of scalding desire on Grady's face.

Respiration ceased as her pulse accelerated, and she felt herself arch upward, meeting Grady's descending mouth halfway.

"Mom, can I buy some more reeds tomorrow . . ."

Eric's voice trailed off as Pamela and Grady jumped guiltily, drawing apart.

Grady looked singularly discomfitted, and Pamela felt her heart sink, fearing a repeat of the afternoon.

But Eric merely turned on his heels and began heading out of the room, mumbling an indistinct, "Excuse me."

"Eric!" Pamela called back. "What is it you need?"

Eric turned reluctantly and answered through the side of his mouth, something he did when upset. "I just came in to ask if I could buy some more reeds. One of them is cracked, and the other doesn't play well in both the high and low registers."

"Sure, no problem. There's a new music store in town. I'm not sure if they have a wide range of supplies for wind instruments, but we'll put it on order if they don't."

"Okay."

"By the way, Eric, you're playing that sax quite well—you can really play after just one year's lessons."

Grady smiled wanly and said, "It sounded quite—quite . . . symphonic. I'm sure the Chicago Symphony Orchestra could use you—in fact, they probably heard you from here."

"Sort of an impromptu audition, wouldn't you say, Grady?" Pamela asked wickedly.

"I didn't disturb you, sir, did I?" Eric asked innocently, his blue eyes gleaming.

"Naw. I'm used to that din . . . dynamite sound." He looked over at Pamela, who was regarding him with barely concealed amusement, and with a frustrated sigh, said, "Well, I guess I'd better get back to bed. Good night."

"Do you need any help?" Eric asked solicitously.

Grady regarded him with narrowed eyes. "No, thanks, Eric. I think you've done enough."

Pamela wished him a sweet "Good night," ignoring the need clamoring inside her tingling flesh.

As Eric tried to make a quick getaway, Pamela said, "Get back in here, young man."

Reluctantly, Eric retraced his steps, and Pamela asked, "You knew Grady had come in here, didn't you?"

"Mom, I do need those reeds," he protested, his blue eyes wide and ingenuous.

"I'm not disputing that. I'm sure it's true. But you came in here to check up on us."

"To check up on him," Eric corrected, then bit his lip. Having let the cat out of the bag, he admitted, "I just don't trust him, Mom. I don't want you to get hurt."

Pamela's stern expression softened, and she said gently, "I appreciate that, Eric. And I love you for caring. But don't you think that at thirty-two, I know what I'm doing and can handle my own decisions, even if they are mistakes? You know, at the hospital they trust me . . ."

"But that's because there you're using your head. Now you're using your heart, and you're not thinking straight."

Pamela sighed, realizing that more and more, her baby was disappearing, and an adult was replacing him.

"Remember how you told me once that I could start dating if I wanted?"

"Yeah, well . . ." Eric was stuck without an answer.

He'd told her that when he was ten, but obviously in the intervening years his sentiments had undergone a radical change. "I remember saying that, but I didn't mean it to apply to Grady. He's too shifty."

"I'll keep that in mind," Pamela told him gravely, and then added brightly, "Now, go to bed and get some rest. And don't let me hear that saxophone again for at least a couple of days."

"Sure thing, Mom," he agreed readily. As he stepped out of the bedroom, he added cheerfully, "No problem there, since I don't have a good reed left."

Pamela threatened him with a pillow, and then lowered the sheet she'd clutched to her bosom when her son had made his unexpected appearance. With a thoughtful expression, she picked up the mystery she'd been reading and resumed the spellbinding story.

The next two days were relatively peaceful, although Eric still played a game of cat and mouse with Grady, zealously guarding his mother from the older man's advances.

Grady, for his own part, was improving daily. Soon he'd be able to make do without the sling. And J.L. was also rapidly recovering—physically, if not in morale; it was a chore trying to keep him confined in the box, and more often than not he would escape and investigate the house like indignant, feathered royalty.

Friday morning, while Eric was helping Grady with his correspondence, Pamela decided to go into the hospital for a few hours.

When she returned, she saw Grady and Eric at the lake. Eric had taken the old but still seaworthy canoe the Westons had left behind into the water. Grady must have helped him, since the wooden canoe was quite heavy.

As Pamela approached with a protesting J.L., Grady turned to look at her.

"Your son's quite a charmer when he stops acting like

Darth Vader and treating me like Simon Legree."

She studied him carefully, and said studiously, "Now that you mention it, there *is* a resemblance—must be the recessive genes."

Grady lunged at her but she evaded him easily, weighed down as he was by his leg cast.

"When are you going to get rid of that bird?"

"You, too? Ye men of little compassion."

"Well, you must admit, even J.L. doesn't look too happy at his enforced captivity," Grady said sententiously.

"And I'm sure you're all broken up about it."

"Enough so that I would recommend setting him free right now."

Pamela laughed and started back to the house, ignoring Grady's advice and ignoring, too, J.L.'s high-pitched squeaking.

After a few steps, she turned around and said, "I'll have a cold lunch ready in half an hour."

"Too late," Grady told her after taking a look at Eric and ascertaining he was still within the canoe. "We already took care of preparing lunch."

Pamela was touched, and smiled her gratitude. "Thanks. I'm really going to enjoy it."

"You sure will. Give Eric a few minutes out there, and then we'll be in to set the table and serve. You just change into something comfy, and put your feet up. The only thing you're allowed to do is serve yourself a drink."

"And you?"

"Okay. You've twisted my arm. You can fix me a drink, too."

That afternoon, Eric helped Grady out again, and Pamela was able to catch up with some household chores.

Grady put in a call to his sons, and Pamela could hear the longing in his voice. He must be really missing them. And they him.

Eric had also heard the wistfulness in Grady's voice, and his antagonism faded somewhat. Her son had always been very sensitive, very compassionate.

When Grady came back to join them for dessert in the living room, Eric started on a lively discussion of baseball greats, having discovered Grady also loved sports.

Grady's gaze met hers across the room, and he nodded imperceptibly. Pamela smiled, her eyes shining, her heart filled with maternal pride.

The moment was soft, yet electric. Pamela felt tuned in to Grady, just as she had when sexual tension had crackled between them.

But this was deeper, an instant of wordless communication in which she felt very close to Grady, with feelings that went beyond passion and emotion.

The moment was shattered when Eric, oblivious to the undercurrent, got up to get some magazines he'd brought with him.

But the warm, all-encompassing feeling remained, enveloping them like nebulous, caressing mist on a moor.

The next morning Pamela came from the utility room, which adjoined the large kitchen, loaded down with freshly laundered clothes for Grady and Eric. She inhaled deeply of the neat, fragrant pile that came up to her chin, and was about to take the stairs to the bedroom when she heard voices coming from the living room.

Excited, *agreeable* voices.

She halted abruptly, almost dropping the bundle of pants, shirts, and briefs, and leaned against the wall, a smile of pleasure and relief lighting her face. Apparently, Grady's sense of loneliness—which Eric could emphasize with all too well—had broken through her son's protective hostility.

"My favorite soccer team is the Sting. They're the greatest, especially Karl-Heinz Granitza and Pato Margetic. I love baseball too, but I thought it was a shame when the Sting won the championship and hardly anyone joined the mayor downtown to congratulate them, because they were so disappointed by the Cubs losing to San Diego."

"Did you go see them?" Grady asked.

"Yeah. I went with Uncle Barrett and Corinna. Mom and Helena had to work, and couldn't get away. But there weren't that many people there."

"I know just how you feel, Eric, but you have to give it time. We've had baseball for over a century, but soccer's only started being popular in the U.S. in the mid-1950's."

"I know." Pamela could hear the disgust in Eric's voice and was glad he'd found a sounding board on one of his passions. The other was basketball. "Many of the boys in school think baseball's the world's greatest sport—"

"But soccer's the number one in the world," Grady agreed with the solemnity of a true sports aficionado. "I know you were too young for the finals in Argentina in '78, but did you make the World Cup Championship in Spain in '82?"

"No," Eric said wistfully. "I didn't even get to see Italy beat Germany on TV. But when I'm old enough, I'm going to attend all the world cups." Then, as a thought struck him, Eric asked curiously, "How come you know so much about soccer and its history, and the New York Cosmos and stuff?"

"I told you. I'm a sports fanatic—particularly about soccer."

As Grady said that, a light blinked on in Pamela's brain, a light that had been dimmed with the shock of Grady's accident, the hectic days following it, and Eric's surprise arrival.

Soccer!

How could she have been so stupid? All the pieces of the puzzle that had roamed restlessly in her mind started coalescing. Grady had once begun to say there were no neighbors; he'd been at her door with a suitcase quite quickly following his hospital escape, and the nearest motel was a good forty minutes away. He had work to catch up on, yet Pamela had never seen the logo on the correspondence. She'd typed in the signature and title, Executive President, then Grady had stamped on the company's letterhead afterward.

And he had maneuvered his way into her house and good graces—or ill graces, she had to admit, as her blood percolated from the seething fury gripping her—and had managed to extend his stay and even to have her take off from work to nurse him.

Soccer.

How could she have been so mush-brained? He'd made no great effort to hide the fact that he was a sports enthusiast—had told her as much. And his name was Talliver: the T of BNT. Bryant, Norris, and Talliver.

But Pamela had never dealt with the Talliver part of the large corporation; she had talked to and received letters and calls only from the Bryant and Norris sides. Even Mr. Lewis had used the umbrella term, BNT, so Pamela had not associated the one with the other.

Maybe her subconscious had prevented her from connecting all the clues. And Grady, astute businessman that he was, had not come clean. He'd taken advantage of her ignorance and sense of guilt and responsibility and, above all, misplaced compassion. Now, in the space of a few days, he'd managed to charm her son, too, or at least he'd gotten Eric to drop his heavy mantle of antagonism.

Pamela realized she had made an accordion of the precisely folded clothes. She unclenched her fingers and wondered in anger and confusion what she would do about Grady. How would Eric feel, knowing Grady had deceived them?

Their conversation went over her head. Pamela felt

as if she were engulfed in a thick, opaque fog. This revelation shouldn't have mattered much—after all, Grady had not actually stolen anything or downright lied. He'd merely kept the truth from her. And if he made an offer now, she would tell him where he could go. Or maybe sic J.L. on him . . . there was someone Grady had not been able to charm.

But as her vision cleared and her pulse lowered to almost normal, the thrumming in her ears diminishing, Pamela realized Grady had indeed stolen something. He'd stolen her trust. She had believed him to be a man of integrity, and the chemistry between them had been instant and undeniable. But it had been more than that. Through their constant sparring—or maybe because of it—there had been a meeting of minds, a pre-knowledge on a deeper, more mysterious level.

Pamela sighed. She was just not lucky with men. Here she'd been admiring the man, appreciating his sensitivity, and reveling in—while yet trying to resist—his air of sensuality, and savoring the underlying gentleness. And he probably didn't even have four boys, she thought in sudden, bursting furor.

He'd been a low-down, rotten, protosimian impostor.

Soccer!

Under Eric's and Barrett's tutelage, she'd begun appreciating the strange, foreign game.

But now Pamela knew she'd never want to hear about it—and would *never, ever* sell her land to make room for a soccer camp!

She quickly ran up the stairs, plopped the clothes on Eric's bed, and descended in double speed. Grady was not spending another minute in her home.

As she entered the living room, Pamela saw Eric lying flat on his stomach in front of the color television set, his head cradled in his palms, and Grady in one of the chairs, his casted leg propped on the ottoman. She noticed Grady was not wearing his shoulder sling.

But it was the noise coming from the TV that caught her attention and made her nerves stand on end—a soccer game.

How appropriate.

Pamela went to stand in front of the console and Eric moved his head like a giraffe, trying to catch any fraction of the picture his mother was obscuring. But Grady immediately looked up at her.

"Was Laurel a sports widow, Grady?"

Grady looked at her, puzzled. As well he should. Her voice was positively dripping sweet acid.

"No, of course not," he answered. "She liked sports, too, but we always did things with the kids on the weekends."

"Oh, you mean the kids are real?" Grady's expression was mystified, and she enlightened him. "I thought maybe they were an invention. You seem to be good at tall tales. And conning people. There was more to your staying here than needing a nurse, wasn't there?"

Grady's features underwent an instant realignment, showing comprehension and guilt. All the proof she needed. With detached interest, Pamela noted that apparently Grady *did* have a conscience. Or was it corporate dismay?

"Mom, I can't see . . ." Eric protested plaintively, his neck cracking from its acrobatic gyrations.

"Then I suggest you go upstairs and watch. You have your small portable in your room."

"But Mom, that's B and W. You know I prefer—"

"Eric, you can still read the scores and see the ball in black and white. Now scoot!"

Eric gave her a surprised look, but when he saw his mother's incensed expression and the green cast to Grady's features, he got to his feet quickly, and scooted.

Grady also got up, his awkward movements failing to elicit Pamela's sympathy this time, although she begrudgingly credited him with some courage. He was going to take this on the chin, like a man.

And she'd love to deliver something to his chin, like a man.

But before she could begin to dispense all the home truths that had accumulated during the quick trip upstairs and back, the doorbell rang.

The warlike chime was followed by other equally stentorian voices. And bellicose barking.

Barking?

Chapter 10

PAMELA OPENED THE door to blaring, piercing pandemonium.

Three adults, four children, and three dogs stood on the threshold—or rather, the adults stood and the children shoved and the dogs leaped and yanked at their leashes.

And what canines! All three looked as though they wouldn't fit through the door, but they could probably leap over the house in a single bound.

Grady stepped forward swiftly, his deep voice cutting temporarily through the tumult, and he quickly made introductions, identifying the older couple as his parents, the tall blonde as his sister, Gabriella, and the four human terrors as Adam, Benji, Craig, and Damien.

Pamela felt somewhat rude keeping the visitors at her doorstep. But she was fuming at Grady's duplicity and was not too kindly disposed to any member of the BNT organization at the moment.

"It's been a pleasure meeting you all," she said politely, moving sideways and opening the door wider for Grady's passage. "You were just leaving, weren't you, Grady? I'll get your suitcase."

"Suitcase?" Gabriella asked quickly, her keen green eyes curious. "What do you—"

She never finished her question as one of the boxers got loose from the chain-reinforced leather leash and the humongous Great Dane gave it swift pursuit.

Pamela had time only to squeal before one dog ran between her legs, lifting her off her feet, while the other finished the job, knocking her off them and onto Grady, who keeled over as if poleaxed.

The boys watched everything avidly, Pamela saw from her advantageous ground-level view, and the adults took a few seconds to recover from appalled shock. They began to run into the house in wake of the four-legged monsters. Pamela registered the last of the dogs escaping from his carelessly held leash.

As the four boys also dashed into the house—everyone seemed to have forgotten her and Grady on the floor—Pamela heard Eric tramping down the stairs, yelling, "Mom, what's happening? Who's invading the house?"

Unerringly, the dogs headed for the kitchen, encountering and demolishing all obstacles along the way, and above all the commotion Pamela heard J.L.'s unmistakable, frantic cry.

"Oh, my God! J.L.!"

Pamela tried to get out of the entanglement of limbs and noticed that Grady did not seem to be in a rush. On the contrary, while she had lain in a nearly catatonic state, Grady had been tranquilly caressing her thighs and derrière!

She slapped his importuning hand away, crying, "Sex fiend!" and stuggled to her feet.

Grady helped her up and Pamela flew toward the source of the ruckus. Adult voices cried out in anger, childish voices in glee, dogs barked in predatory chase, and J.L. squawked with pure, unadulterated terror.

Pamela squealed to a stop on the wet-looking, recently cleaned floor, and covered her mouth in horror.

A pathetic sight greeted her.

The homemade German sausages she'd been preparing this morning were undulating throughout the kitchen. The Great Dane and the larger boxer each had an end and they playfully pulled and tossed the sausage links into the air, batted them with their massive heads, and caught them again.

Dear Lord! Did even the dogs play soccer in this confounded family?

Her momentary paralysis fled as she saw a feather-shedding J.L. bolting to the windowsill with the remaining boxer trying to jump onto the counter and almost succeeding. Galvanized into action, Pamela saw the adults peripherally as she ran to the rescue. They were trying to remove the two sausage-pulling dogs—two women on the boxer, the man on the Great Dane—and as Pamela approached the eye of the storm, she saw that the boys, instead of helping, were egging the third dog into rapacious hunting.

"Boys!" Grady's voice cut through the unholy din.

But although his sons began backing away from the boxer, one of them yelled a last encouraging war cry. "Go get him, Miss Marple!"

Miss Marple?

Pamela threw herself into the fray and pushed through the four boys to boost herself onto the counter. J.L. had obviously had the best of incentives to resume flying: self-preservation.

Behind her, Pamela heard several disjointed phrases.

"Come on, Charlie Chan!"

"Damn it, Mr. Moto!"

"Boys, get Miss Marple away—"

"Grady, how could this have happened..."

"Sweet heaven! Look at this mess!"

"Poor Mrs. Shaw..."

And through the babble, Pamela heard Eric's voice, clear as a bell, bellowing in manly tones, "Don't worry, Mom. The police are on their way."

Everyone stopped, even the dogs... as if the magic mention of police were universally understood. And feared.

Pamela sagged with a shaking J.L. in her arms and moaned, "That's all I need!"

Grady's strong good arm went around her, bolstering her liquefied body as her gaze sweeped about the disaster-struck kitchen, surveying the cataclysm.

"What do you think, Claude? Should we throw them in the slammer?"

The taller officer looked at his short, angular partner and said, "Well, Matt, I just don't know. Seems to me there's been plenty of damage here. Vandalism, disturbing the peace, inciting a riot... Those hounds should go to the calaboose, too."

"Oh, no, please!" said one of the boys whom Pamela tentatively identified as either Benji or Craig. "They're innocent. You can't take Charlie Chan, Mr. Moto, or Miss Marple!"

"Come again?" Claude asked.

"The dogs, officer," Grady explained. "My boys are crazy about private eyes." He looked toward where a shell-shocked Pamela leaned against the refrigerator and said, "I don't think Mrs. Shaw is going to press charges. And Eric can be forgiven for jumping the gun. It did look like Attila the Hun and Genghis Khan had joined forces in here."

Pamela looked at the ruin that was her kitchen and

studied Grady speculatively. He quickly added, "Of course, we'll pay for any damages."

"And what about the sausages?" she demanded. "Do you know how long they take to make? Are you willing to prepare those from scratch, too?"

Gabriella, obviously taking pity on her brother, said, "It's his birthday today. That's why we all drove up with the kids: to surprise him."

"I think I can do without surprises for quite a spell," Grady muttered.

"Well, as it's his birthday . . ." Pamela began. She saw the boys hanging on to her every word, worried most, she knew, about the fate of their canine accomplices. "We'll let bygones be bygones. I'm sorry to put you through so much trouble, officers."

"That's all right, ma'am," Claude said magnanimously. "It was a slow day."

Pamela saw the officers to the door and returned to the living room, where the Tallivers and Eric were congregated. Pamela saw Grady had put his boys to straightening overturned tables and picking up pieces of china and glass.

When he saw her, Grady told her grimly, "I'll have those replaced, too. Hope they didn't hold sentimental value?"

Pamela looked around and saw that the hand-painted Japanese musical figurine her parents had gotten her for her thirteenth birthday and the crystal bowl that had been a shower present from Paul were still intact.

"No. Fortunately, the pieces that I most care about seem to have come through unscathed."

Grady smiled, relieved, and turned toward Eric, who was looking stunned and holding Jonathan Livingston.

"Mom, Dad, Gabriella, this is Pamela Shaw's son, Eric. The sea gull he's holding is Jonathan Livingston."

His parents and sister didn't bat an eyelid and after

all, why should they? Not after four two-legged horrors and three four-legged ones—Marple, Moto, and Chan.

"And these are my parents, Georgette and Irving Talliver, and my sister Gabriella." Pointing to his disheveled, sausage and flour-covered darlings, he said in much the same manner as Captain Von Trapp in *The Sound of Music,* "And these . . . are my angels: Adam, Benji, Craig, and Damien." Pamela saw that the child she supposed was Benji or Craig was actually Craig; although a year younger, he was an inch taller.

"I'm really glad you've decided to sell my brother your property," Gabriella said with a friendly smile. Pamela's answering smile stiffened. "He's always had a dream of starting a soccer camp—"

"Gabriella—" Grady tried to warn.

"Ms. Talliver," Pamela began, overriding Grady.

Grady corrected her. "Mrs. Norris."

Pamela's glance quickly flew to Grady and the older Tallivers exchanged puzzled glances.

"Mrs. Norris?"

"That's right. My husband was Malcolm Norris, one of the partners. When he died nine months ago, I took over for him and I've been spelling Grady while he's been scouting for his soccer camp."

"Oh, I'm sorry," Pamela said, her gaze practically perforating Grady. She was sorry for Gabriella's loss—she seemed a nice woman. But Grady . . . well, the word nice did not apply in his case.

"You didn't know?" Gabriella asked, confused. "But Grady told me he'd be contacting you personally after Mr. Lewis, the man I sent while Grady was out of the country, didn't seem to make any headway with you . . ."

Grady intervened with a decisive tone. "Why don't we leave business until Monday? After all, today is my thirty-eighth . . ."

"I didn't realize you were *that* old," Eric put in with renewed bellicosity.

Grady sighed, and Pamela was almost sorry for him.

But she felt that the older Tallivers and the boys should not be subjected to this private war. She addressed them, "Perhaps you'd care for a refreshment before going back to Grady's place? I have some drinks that should be safe and sound in the refrigerator. I hope."

The Tallivers, both tall and fair and charming, laughed. "We hope so, too, my dear," Irving said. "Any chance of a beer?"

"I'm afraid not. But I do have some wine or schnapps."

"A spritzer sounds just about right," Georgette said.

"Yes, and after that we'll help you clean up," Gabriella offered.

"We can handle it ourselves," Eric put in belligerently.

Gabriella looked taken aback, and although Pamela wanted to regard her as a corporate sneak, she found that Gabriella's openness and warmth precluded such an attitude.

"What my son means," Pamela broke into the awkward silence, "is that you should go on celebrating Gradys's birthday. We'll clean up the kitchen later."

Gabriella smiled uncertainly and the Tallivers politely. The boys seemed divided into two camps. Adam and Craig looked hostile, while Eric, Benji and Damien appeared indifferent. Luckily, the dogs were temporarily subdued—although J.L. kept a leery, beady eye on them.

As for Grady, he had an enigmatic look on his face. Pamela sighed and said, "Shall we leave the war zone?"

As the Talliver clan was about to depart, Georgette asked, "You will come to the party later tonight? We stopped at the supermarket on the edge of town and will have a veritable feast."

"Oh, I'm afraid I can't, Mrs. Talliver," Pamela protested. "I have an awful lot of work to catch up on."

"Please, do come," Gabriella cajoled warmly. "You can spare a couple of hours—even hospital administrators have to rest."

Pamela looked from Gabriella to Grady, wondering

what he had told his conclusion-jumping sister. Gabriella quickly added, "Grady told us something about you. We just didn't know you had so graciously extended your hospitality."

Eric snorted, and Pamela was quite tempted to dispel all confusion right now and reveal what a smooth, slithering operator Grady really was. Graciously extend her hospitality, indeed!

But a look at the courteous Tallivers and the friendly Gabriella stopped her. After all, business was business. And a birthday, no matter that it be for a conniving charmer, was an occasion for rejoicing and merrymaking.

Smothering the hot words on her tongue, Pamela cast Grady a jaundiced look and said, "Maybe I'll stop in for a little while . . ."

"Please do," Gabriella jumped in quickly as if afraid Pamela would change her mind. "It will help us make some amends—however slight—for the inconvenience we've caused you. And bring Eric, of course. Seven o'clock."

Pamela saw them out and heaved a sigh of relief as they began to climb into a large, late-model van.

Just as she was to close the door, one of the little sweethearts turned around, aimed a slingshot, and—with deadly accuracy—released it.

The large stone struck Pamela squarely on her shapely derrière, and she yelped in mingled pain and outrage.

"You okay, Mom?" Eric asked, coming up quickly behind her.

Pamela forced a smile onto her humor-resistant lips. "Yes. Guess I miscalculated and hit my fanny on the door." She didn't want her son to know what had happened, or World War III would commence tonight.

Lacing her arm about Eric's waist, she asked as they went toward the infamous kitchen. "Do you mind very much going over tonight, Eric? It would have been impolite to refuse."

"You're just too nice, Mom," Eric said. "You let

everyone steamroller you. You should take some assertiveness-training classes."

"I did," Pamela protested laughingly. She stopped before entering the kitchen and put her hands on the boy's shoulders. "If you don't want to go, son, we won't. I didn't realize you hated the idea so much."

"I don't, Mom," Eric said. "I just hate the thought of your being manipulated, first taking care of Grady, then helping him with his work, now his relatives . . ." He ruffled his mother's already mussed hair and said, "You take in all kinds of strays. You just can't say no."

"Maybe so," Pamela agreed. "But I'd like to think that when I need something some day, someone will be there for me, too."

Eric took her gentle comment with a smile and said, "All right. I'll try to combine cynicism with a pair of rose-colored glasses. Just watch out for Grady Talliver, though."

"Will do," Pamela said as her son held the kitchen door open for her. She felt more friend than mother at the moment—and it was a warm feeling. "Oh, before I forget . . . I better call Helena. When I called her to let her know you'd gotten here safely, she said she'd telephone tonight."

"Okay. Can I take some of my electronic games with me, Mom? Some of my cartridges are compatible with Benji's home computer, which he brought with him."

Pamela shook her head, smiling at the quick networking of children. Even in the middle of bedlam, they could communicate about shared passions—namely, computers and punk rock.

Pamela saw the old Jentzen place looked pretty much the same on the outside as it had before BNT had acquired it. Obviously, Grady had not had the time to effect any repairs on the rambling, large, rather dilapidated three-story house.

Every light seemed to be on, imbuing the house with old country warmth. As Pamela and Eric approached the house, two distinct sounds seemed to be competing within: Heavy Metal and Chopin.

Eric looked at her, grinning, and Pamela grinned back. Her son was sporting tailored navy slacks and a light blue shirt—which was rapidly becoming wrinkled from the pile of games he'd brought along. His neatly combed hair was already surrendering to the night wind, and Pamela was glad she'd put her own tresses in a short, swinging ponytail, or her hair would have been blown away by the strong breeze on the leisurely walk to Grady's place.

Pamela knocked on the door, and one of the boys answered. Craig. The iniquitous inciter of big Miss Marple, and probably the slingshot sharpster as well.

Eric went in, humming to the Hall and Oates tune "Private Eyes" emanating from the deep bowels of the house. Pamela could definitely feel eyes watching her—but not with welcome. She hung back and smiling sweetly, asked, "Is it safe to come in? Or should I watch for any boobytraps?"

Craig's smile was angelic, but his gaze was demonic. "See for yourself. You're not welcome here."

Pamela looked up to see Gabriella approaching. "Good evening," she said, smiling warmly. "Glad you could make it." Putting her arms about her nephew's shoulders—Pamela got the impression Grady's sister was trying to protect her from the evils of the innocent-looking cherub—she asked, "Everything all right?"

Craig's gaze was now benign and his smile guileless. "I was just telling Mrs. Shaw that she should feel right at home."

Gabriella gave him a quick hug, obviously wanting to believe in a miraculous change of behavior, and said, relief threading her voice, "Why, that's real nice, sweetheart. Make sure you and your brothers keep Eric entertained, okay?"

"Okay," Craig said, scampering off. He stopped at the end of the hallway and, turning, gave Pamela such a look of malevolence that she felt transported to the Amityville Horror.

Determined to hold her own with the little fiend, Pamela gave him a jaunty wave and resplendent smile, and had the satisfaction of seeing Craig scowl.

"May I talk to you for a minute?" Gabriella requested. "Grady's on the phone right now—something urgent's come up in Ohio—and I probably won't get another chance."

Pamela looked at her curiously. "Sure."

Gabriella said, "This way," and led her into a darkly paneled library off the living room.

As they sat down on a lavender velvet sofa, Gabriella began, "I'm sorry I assumed so much about you and your property. Grady had told me you were opposed to selling it when he called us shortly after your . . . your run-in, but he never did tell us he was staying over at your place. And tonight, we went to Grady's house first and found it unlived in, and then you mentioned the suitcase . . ."

"So you jumped to the conclusion that your brother had mixed some fun with business, right?" Pamela supplied as Gabriella's voice trailed off. Shaking her head, she smiled and said, "He probably wanted to maintain his anonymity until he'd softened me up."

"No! Not at all. My brother might be infuriating, overbearing, and creatively persuasive at times, but he wouldn't mix business with pleasure."

Pamela smiled faintly. "Staunch, loyal defense. Do I detect more than a business conversation going on here?" she asked quizzically.

"You do," Gabriella confessed candidly. "I know I was very persistent about acquiring your property, Pamela—may I call you Pamela?" At Pamela's nod, Gabriella continued, "But I really wanted my brother to fulfill his dream, one he's had since he was a college student. That's why I sent Jay Lewis to try to expedite things."

"You were on the right track. Quite persistent, your Mr. Lewis."

"Yes, well, we didn't know how important your house was to you—or that you'd left Illinois to gamble on a new life in practically the back of beyond because you fell in love with that home."

"I fell in love with the house, the area, and the job," Pamela corrected quietly. "But I couldn't have bought the house—wouldn't even have known of it—were it not for my job." Pamela straightened the fold of her raspberry, tulip-hemmed dress, and asked, "Does this mean BNT is withdrawing its offer and generally ceasing to make a nuisance of itself?"

Before Gabriella could answer, Grady limped into the room, barely making use of the crutch.

"There you are. I was wondering who had spirited away my guest."

Gabriella stood up, not bothering to hide the annoyance visible on her elegant, expressive features. "Ah, brother dear. Always sneaking up on people," she teased. Smoothing the pants of her black velvet pantsuit, she said, "She's all yours." At Grady's voracious smile, Gabriella added with a wicked grin, "I'd tell you to watch out for him, Pamela, but since he's lived on your own territory, I imagine you've got my dear brother figured out."

"Quite well," Pamela responded dryly.

"Always misunderstood," Grady said with a wounded air, and Gabriella looked at the ceiling with a "Give me patience, Lord" look.

Gabriella delivered her parting shot as she left the

room. "I'm afraid we understand you only too well."

Grady walked over to the couch and told Pamela with quiet urgency, "Listen, we need to talk. And we can't do it here. Do you want to go for a drive?"

"But it's your party, and Eric has your presents—"

"Forget the presents! I have to go back to Ohio tomorrow—Gabriella doesn't know it yet, but she'll be staying here with the boys. And I don't want this hanging over our heads for a week."

"I don't know what you mean. I told you I won't sell . . ."

"The hell with the property right now! I'm talking about us." Pamela started at his vehemence, and Grady leaned forward, gazing intently into her eyes. "Let's clear the air, shall we? We owe each other that much."

Pamela opened her mouth to tell Grady that neither of them owed the other a thing when she remembered how devastated she'd felt when she'd stumbled onto the truth earlier today. He was right; they had to discuss it. She knew Grady felt *something* for her, and she'd never forgive herself if she didn't give him a chance to explain. After all, business rivals, fierce competitors, met, courted, loved, every day. She could at least listen to him.

Pamela lifted her gaze to meet his and saw him looking at her with longing, tenderness . . . and raw need.

"What about the party?" she asked. "And dinner . . ."

"I'll tell my parents we're going for a drive. They can set dinner back. The boys are allowed to stay up late tonight." Giving her a gold key ring, he told her, "Why don't you go bring the car to the door? It's the maroon Mercedes. I'll go find my parents and will be out shortly."

Pamela got her purse from the table in the entrance hall and went outside to bring the car up.

Grady soon joined her. As he slid carefully into the passenger seat, she asked, "How are you feeling?"

"One hundred percent better, Doc," he told her, adding

casually, "Why don't you drive back to your house? It's a beautiful evening, and we'll be undisturbed there."

Pamela's brows raised, but she didn't object. He was right. It was a lovely night, and if they went over to her place, they could get back soon.

Grady led her toward the lake, using his crutch dexterously while keeping his right arm about her. "Come on," he told her as he steered her toward the hammock.

As they sat down, Grady discarded the crutch and leaned back, his silk shirt gleaming white in the dark of night. "I'd like to apologize for not having told you who I was after I found out who you were," he said. "I'd just gotten in the night before our momentous meeting, and had gone for an early run with the idea of tackling you later in the morning."

"Instead, I tackled you."

"With a vengeance," Grady said, chuckling. "In the hospital, I figured out you had to be my neighbor. So I decided to show up on your doorstep, mad at you for having taken off, and saying the least you could do was take care of me. And initially, I admit, I thought it would be easier to work on you on your own turf."

"And get in some fun on the side?"

Grady took her hand in his. "No. I didn't want to convince you that way. That's what I wanted you to know—and believe. My business and my personal feelings are two distinct entities. Yes, I want your land, even now, even after knowing you've fulfilled your dream. Because I want to fulfill mine. And I have some idea of a compromise . . ."

Pamela shook her head. "No, don't. I haven't changed my mind. And I won't, no matter how you try to sweet-talk me."

"Well, that's certainly laying it on the line. But I also want you to know right now that I'm going to keep trying to convince you—in plain daylight, of course."

Pamela sighed and said, "Grady, I just don't think this is a good idea. We're bound to get hurt. We're at odds, and there's no way—"

Grady put a finger on her lips and said, "Pamela, we don't have long. I have to go back and conclude some deals. We can discuss this at some later date. What couldn't wait was the fact that you believed I'd accepted your hospitality and tried to befriend Eric just for the sake of a soccer camp. I'm admitting I originally went to your house with all sorts of stratagems—but they went out the window the moment you tried to get me up off that couch."

"Which reminds me," she asked him, her eyes glittering. "Was that for real, or a put-on?"

"I tell all under torture," Grady said, his grin a flash of white against his bronzed skin. "Care to try me?"

Pamela looked at him, his gray eyes silver and steady as they met hers, and when she didn't say anything, Grady asked, uncertainty and anxiety lacing his voice, "Do you believe me, Pamela? Do you believe that my attraction for you has nothing to do with the blasted camp?"

Pamela held his gaze a moment longer, and then nodded slowly. Grady moved forward, setting the hammock into a slight swing, and kissed her forehead softly. Next, his butterfly touch alighted on her eyelids and then brushed against her nose, cheeks, and chin, finally settling on her mouth with sweet poignancy.

The kiss was light, exploratory, at first. The touch of two friends who enjoy each other. Then, slowly, imperceptibly, the kiss changed in texture and pressure, becoming a lover's caress. Their lips touched, met, rubbed, tingled from the meeting, until Grady cupped the back of her head and opened his mouth over hers.

Pamela parted her lips eagerly, welcoming the too-long-denied exchange. Grady took her lower lip into his mouth and gently bit it. Pamela moaned and her hands rose of their own volition to his shoulders, clutching in sensual agony. Then he released the tender, swollen flesh and thrust his tongue inside. Pamela met him with hungry aggressiveness and captured him, carrying the willing captive into the hot, dark confines of her mouth.

The kiss continued, unending, growing in intensity until Pamela felt as if she knew every taste and texture of Grady's mouth. But he pulled away, resting his damp forehead on hers, gasping in air with desperate gulps. Pamela's own breathing was heavy, and she felt her knees tremble.

Grady lifted his head and looked down at her. "I wish I could tell you I hadn't brought you out here to seduce you, but considering it was here that I first got to taste and feel you, I can't say that with any certainty. Consciously, I didn't, but my subconscious may very well have had other urgings."

"Trying to disarm me with your honesty?" Pamela asked, lifting one hand to caress the strong neck that looked so dark against the pristine collar.

Grady captured her hand and took it to his mouth. "No. One thing you can believe. I'll always be honest with you. No subterfuge, no lies, between us."

He lowered himself slowly onto the hammock and pulled her toward him gently, letting her make the final choice.

Pamela protested, "You're crazy," but allowed him to lower her against his chest. "Your leg's still broken."

"But I've regained use of my left hand. It's a bit rusty, but it'll do in a pinch." He illustrated his words by using his hand to lower the starburst strap of one shoulder, and buried his head on the opposite, bared one.

"Pamela, I want to make love to you. I can't wait any longer, and I'm going to make love to you even if I fall off and break my other leg in the process."

The husky timbre to his voice played on her skin, warming the flesh that the night air was cooling. His lips followed the line of her collarbone, and Pamela could smell his own distinct scent, woodsy and fresh and mingling with the fragrance of early summer.

She pressed against him with answering need, and she felt his body harden beneath hers as his hands lifted her skirt above her knees. His smooth, deep muscles felt heavenly beneath her softer form.

"Pamela?" One of his hands left her thighs and cradled her chin. "Am I going too fast for you?"

A wave of tenderness washed over her. Although he could have ignited her like a match thrown on dry timber, he was willing to subjugate his own yearning. She liked his gentleness, his consideration. And he was not going too fast—on the contrary, not fast enough. Three years was a long time, and sex had always been good with Trevor—that had never been the problem.

"No, you're not rushing me," she whispered.

She planted an elbow on either side of him, and Grady lifted both legs onto the hammock. As he grabbed her waist and pulled her up so he could push the bodice down, Pamela laughed deep in her throat, feeling the enchantment of the night weave about her, the slight breeze tickling her bare back, bringing the scents of the lake and summer flowers and pungent trees to her . . .

Grady raised his head and buried his face in her throat, echoing her thoughts. "Lord, you smell good." One hand went down to her thigh to push her dress up to her waist, while the other curved about her neck. "I want to devour you. You feel like silk."

Pamela felt her insides tighten as his hands caressed the gentle curve of her sides and his lips left a lei of kisses about her neck, then settled on her life pulse, where he suckled her flesh and licked it maddeningly.

She gasped as he bared his teeth and took quick nips.

Her body shivered under the onslaught of tactile and olfactory sensations and she surrendered the tight control she'd kept over herself.

One of her hands left the hammock and Grady supported her shoulder as she began to attack his own clothes, opening his shirt with shaking fingers and unbuckling his belt.

Grady inhaled sharply and slid one hand to her back, unfastening her sheer, strapless bra. Then, as she began to unzip his pants, he ran his hands down her sides, past her waist and to her thighs, ascending once more to cup her rounded buttocks underneath the folds of her skirt. Pamela dropped kisses on his slightly damp neck, and when she administered a sharp nip of her own, Grady groaned and sought her mouth. The long, drugging kiss took her to the edge of abandon, and when Grady pulled away to allow her a gulp of sweet night air, Pamela slid upward on the hammock, her breasts positioned directly over his mouth.

His hand tightened on her bottom, his fingers closing and opening, pulling her against his belly even as he kneaded her flesh. His mouth opened over one breast and almost engulfed it.

Pamela closed her eyes in ecstasy. Wishing to return some of the pleasure she was receiving, she caressed his chest with her free hand.

Grady sucked on her breast and Pamela's stomach turned into a live coil of need. She scratched lightly at his chest, and when his mouth moved to the other breast, again almost swallowing it into his moist, searing depths, Pamela moaned in sensual delirium.

She could no longer support herself, her body melting even as her nipples hardened into aching points and her breasts swelled. When Grady began to tug at her panties, Pamela lifted her weakened, trembling body.

"Grady, wait. I want to feel you, to pleasure you . . ."

"Sweetheart, I'm so pleasured right now I'm about to

burst." The panties slipped down her legs and were lost in the depths of the hammock.

"We'll look a bit disheveled at the party, won't we?" Pamela asked as Grady bunched her dress around her hips.

"No more than the boys will," he answered thickly, and began to lift her onto him.

Worry cutting through her fervid haze, Pamela said, "Your leg . . ."

"We'll manage," he assured her raspily, his breathing labored as he edged closer to the middle of the hammock. "Lift your hips," he instructed as his hands closed about her waist.

Pamela complied, desire firing her blood and quickening her pulse to a hammerbeat.

As he positioned her, his mouth closed over her left breast. Pamela gasped, and when he pressed her hips downward, she felt the velvety tip of his manhood against her aching moistness.

But even though she was hot and ready, his entrance was a sensual shock and her muscles tightened before he could enter her completely.

He kissed an engorged nipple which hardened even more as a nocturnal breeze dried the moisture on the tumescent crest, and he spoke against her flesh, "Relax. Open yourself to me."

He buried his head in the scented valley between her breasts and held himself back, letting her adjust herself to their contact.

Pamela levered herself, raising her hips and then lowering them slowly, careful of Grady's cast. Grady's hands left her hips and ran down her body in long, sweeping strokes, his head lifting to brush soft kisses against her breasts, taking small nibbles of the warm mounds.

The tenseness left Pamela's body as Grady's hands soothed her and kindled a fierce flame once more. She bit her lip and pushed downward, still alert enough to notice Grady's iron control over his own passion.

She accepted him completely, feeling both an emotional and physical hunger. Closing about his pulsating manhood, she started to move rhythmically. Grady continued his slow, languorous caresses until Pamela began to breath raggedly, and then his hands returned to her hips.

"Hold on," he told her as he slid onto his left side, taking her with him. He positioned one leg above her waist and thrust powerfully.

All speech and rational thought fled then, and Pamela blindly sought his mouth.

Their lips met and clung, their tongues touched and dueled, and the unusual position elevated the eroticism to a new level.

No more did Pamela experience the ebb and flow of passion. Her hands stroked Grady's back and chest and she thrust even harder against him.

Their hands and lips and bodies pushed them toward a quick, shattering culmination. When it came, Grady's penetration met her innermost being, and their bodies shuddered in unison. Pamela hid her face against Grady's shoulder to stifle her cry of fulfillment, while his hand closed about her breast as his own groan reverberated in the clear summer night...

Never had Pamela felt more joyful or contented.

Chapter 11

"YOU SEEM TO have enjoyed your drive," Gabriella told them with a straight face and a teasing glint in her keen green eyes as they quickly roved over Grady and Pamela's slightly disheveled dress.

Grady put his hand protectively around Pamela's waist and ushered her into the foyer. "Where is everyone?" he demanded.

"Sitting down to dinner. We thought you two had forgotten all about it," his sister answered as she led the way to the dining room. Looking over her shoulder and apparently taking in Grady's tender gesture and Pamela's heightened color, she continued, "I figured I'd better meet you at the door—the older boys might have made mincemeat of your . . . casual appearance."

Grady tightened his grip on Pamela and, although she blushed deeply, she countered spiritedly, "It was windy outside." As Gabriella turned to look at her and raised plainly disbelieving eyebrows, Pamela added, "Well, changing would have looked even more incriminating."

Grady smiled down at her. "As I'm the birthday boy, I think I can celebrate the most enjoyable way. And Pamela is certainly old enough to choose for herself." The intimate look he gave her transmitted to Pamela how much their lovemaking had meant—it had been intense, yes, but also full of a quiet gentleness.

Pamela walked into the living room on cloud nine, and proceeded to enjoy the lavish birthday dinner of shrimp cocktail, steak, and a mushroom and spinach salad, Grady's favorite.

Afterward, the children gathered around the huge, ice-cream cake shaped like a soccer ball while everyone sang "Happy Birthday" and watched Grady blow out the candles and cut the cake.

Then Grady was heaped with presents: old staples like ties and socks as well as more imaginative gifts such as a portable radio-TV to catch games on the road, and the lastest in computer technology—a computer the size of a legal letter.

Pamela felt the warmth emanating from Grady's family and reflected that this was something she'd been searching for all her life. She looked on wistfully, glad Eric had been accepted so readily and unreservedly by Grady's sons.

She noticed with a start that Grady was unwrapping her presents. Pamela had had a hard time choosing them with such short notice, and had not felt it right to get Grady anything overly expensive. So from Eric and herself she had given Grady a Mark Cross pen set, as well as a more individualized gift that was contained in a huge box.

Grady enlisted the help of his sons to open the large box. Damien shouted with glee, "Hey, this is fun!"

Adam, the oldest, just looked at her scornfully. Pamela

knew he looked on her as a threat, but could not do anything about it. Out of the corner of her eye she saw Craig trying to back out of the room unnoticed, but obviously Georgette Talliver also had an eagle eye, because she moved slowly, almost imperceptibly, to intercept her grandson, putting a loving but restraining hand on his shoulder.

Gabriella began to gather the profusion of gaily-colored paper, and said, laughing, "Hey, I can use this to wallpaper the company apartment."

Finally, Grady reached the last package and opened it. His eyes widened as he saw its contents: a real soccer ball, as well as a smaller one designed to hold memos and office supplies such as paperclips and rubber bands in its beehive-shaped cubicles.

Grady's eyes sought hers, and his look told her more than his sincere, simple words. "Thank you. Am I to understand I'm forgiven?"

All eyes converged on Pamela, and she smiled. "Well, let's say I wanted you to enjoy your birthday."

"Oh, I am enjoying it," Grady said softly, and Pamela noticed the glances exchanged between his parents and sister.

But Craig was obviously not ruled by good manners and etiquette. Loudly, he asked, "May I be excused? There's something I want to see on TV."

The older Tallivers looked ready to say something, and Grady frowned, but he let the moment pass, saying only with quiet authority, "You can watch TV all summer, son. I think I would like you around to help me celebrate my birthday."

Sullen and shamefaced, Craig joined his three brothers, and Gabriella broke in with characteristic cheer, "How about helping me clean this mess, and then we can all play some games?"

The boys complied, the occasion obviously making them more accommodating than usual. Pamela got up, feeling she had intruded on the family long enough, and began making her excuses.

"Please, won't you stay a while longer?" Mrs. Talliver asked.

"We really have to go," Pamela answered, smiling. "I appreciate your inviting us, and I'd like to thank you for the wonderful dinner."

"I'll go get my stuff, Mom," Eric told her, following Adam out of the room. Benji quickly followed, but Pamela noticed that Craig stayed behind, his hostile, unsettling gaze beaming on her.

"I'll see you to the door," Grady told her, and Pamela said good-bye to the family, going to the front door to wait for Eric.

"Do you want to take my car?" Grady asked, his hand caressing her cheek as they stood in the doorway.

"No, I'll be fine. I enjoy walking, especially in the evening."

"Wish I could accompany you," Grady said, tapping his leg. "But I don't think I'd get very far with this, and I'd rather not break any more bones. Casts can be an awful nuisance in certain circumstances."

Pamela smiled, and said huskily, "I think you acquitted yourself quite well."

Lowering his head, Grady whispered in her ear, "You ain't seen nothin' yet." His hand went to the back of her neck, which he'd found to be ultrasensitive, and he began to work unspeakable magic on her responsive skin. "I'll call you tomorrow, okay?"

Pamela nodded, speech beyond the realm of possibility at the moment and unnecessary. Grady was communicating quite well nonverbally.

She was snapped out of her sensual reverie by Gabriella's deliberately raised voice. "Pamela, do you want to meet me for lunch tomorrow? Bring Eric, of course."

Grady groaned and stepped back.

"Sorry, Gabriella, but I won't be able to tomorrow,"

Pamela called. "I've gotten a bit behind at work." Grady's hand tightened on hers, which he had against his chest, in response to her gentle reminder of his duplicity. "Could we make it toward the end of the week?"

"All right. I've been drafted to mind the four horrors while Grady goes back to Ohio to take care of some urgent business. Just give me a call on a more definite time, okay?"

"Will do," Pamela promised.

"Good night, then. I'll leave you two lovebirds to say good-bye alone. And don't worry, I'll make sure the coast is clear."

Grady shook his head, and Pamela asked, "Is she always so forthright?"

"Depressingly so. When we were children she always got us in the doghouse because she couldn't dissemble. We could have gotten away with a lot more if only she'd been—"

"Like her older brother?" Pamela asked softly. "A pro at deceit?"

Grady leaned one hand above her head, and placed the other one on her hip. The outside lights had been turned off, and moonlight reached them as they stood half-in, half-out of the house.

"Originally, I came to Michigan to offer you a business proposition," he told her. "I did try to manipulate all factors in my favor—but the land is no longer the issue between us. Not the main one."

Pamela moved away from the doorway and from the tender imprisonment of Grady's arms. Too much had happened in one day, and emotions were still running high. In a way, she was glad Grady was leaving. It would give them both some breathing space. And time to think things through more coolly, more logically, without the thought-paralyzing attraction their proximity induced.

Grady dropped his hand from her hip, and as he moved away, Pamela felt capable of breathing freely once more.

Marching and trampling to rival an elephant herd reached their ears long before five healthy bodies appeared.

"Thanks for inviting me, Grady. I really had a great time," Eric said quite cordially. Pamela put her arm about his shoulders as he stepped to her side, and she experienced a wave of maternal pride.

"I'm glad, Eric."

"Dad, can we walk them to their house?" Adam asked. "We could help Eric carry his stuff."

"Oh, no," Pamela said quickly. "That won't be necessary."

"Yes, Dad. Adam and I want to talk to Eric some more," Craig said.

"We'll be back right away," Adam insisted.

Pamela could tell Grady was suspicious. *She* definitely was . . . and she'd only known the boys a short time. And now Grady was in a bind. He obviously wanted to protect her from whatever scheme the boys were planning. But he did not want to appear to be protecting her, nor to deny the boys the chance to get to know her better on the long shot that they didn't have anything nefarious in mind.

Pamela decided the issue for him.

"That would be lovely, boys. It'll give us a chance to get to know each other better."

"What for?" Craig said rudely. Pamela saw Eric stiffen and approach Craig, but before her son could say anything, the younger boy added quickly, "I mean, we'll be around from now on." The way he said it, it sounded ominous, and there was an uncomfortable silence. Craig, feeling his father's unrelenting gaze on him, added, "What I mean is, I just don't think you'll like us. My mother was a real practical joker, and she enjoyed a lot of fun, and kidding around . . . and things . . ."

Craig wound down, apparently aware he'd only muddled things. Grady, with admirable restraint, said gently, "I think if I've taught you something in life, Craig, it's that everyone's different. There is no perfect model on this earth—we all have to learn to tolerate each other and rejoice in those differences, and ultimately learn to respect each other."

Eric dispelled the awkward moment that followed by saying, "Mom, can we go? My arms are getting numb from holding this stuff."

The Talliver boys were obviously relieved to have gotten off so lightly—Grady's little warning had clearly been meant for all of them, not just Craig—and Pamela quickly said good-bye.

Grady did not try to touch or kiss her again, but merely reiterated that he'd be calling her the following day. After warning Adam and Craig to come straight home after walking Eric and Pamela home, Grady closed the door in back of them.

Adam helped Eric carry some of his things, and Pamela led the way to her home. She knew Craig was lurking somewhere, but she'd be damned if she'd look around, letting him know she was the slightest bit nervous.

She picked up the pace of her striding, and within a few minutes they were in sight of home. As she hurried up the front, flower-strewn path, Pamela heaved a sigh of relief.

And knew it was premature just moments later, when Adam bid Eric good-bye and Craig materialized lurking near the side of the house.

Pamela went into the house, asking Eric to put on some water for tea while she went upstairs and took a quick shower.

As she walked into the bathroom, she did get a shower. A cold, unexpected one.

She stood rigidly angry for a minute, looking up at the bucket ingeniously suspended and creatively engineered to let her have it.

Pamela knew the trick had been prepared earlier that day—sometime between her leaving the house and dinnertime. The kids had been very much in evidence after that. And the fact the water was still icy cold showed the boys' ingenuity: They'd filled it with ice cubes to ensure a frigid bath.

While water dripped down her face and neck and her once-elegant dress drooped and clung to her chilled body, Pamela reflected that the boys certainly did not want her around. They were making that fact very clear.

Yet it was also perfectly clear that they were not hardened delinquents or unnecessarily cruel. Since they were able to get into the house—Pamela had not secured all the windows that evening before attending the party, something she intended doing from now on—they could also have dreamed up a more devastating stunt. But they were not trying to hurt her. Merely to warn her and scare her off.

Methodically stripping, Pamela put a large bath towel about her while stewing about Craig's appearance from the side of the house. That could have been a ploy to lull her into a sense of security—or to get her to believe that she could be expecting a sneak attack from that quarter. But Pamela was convinced there was more to it than that. Without hesitation, she tiptoed across the large, icy puddle in the huge yellow bathroom, and approached the bathtub.

And there they were. The cutest little frogs Pamela had seen this side of childhood, happily burping and hopping about her shiny golden bathtub.

Smiling with relief, she secured the towel around the upper swell of her breasts, and got another towel to evict the jumpy little intruders.

After a lot of sliding and chasing, she was able to dispose of them without Eric's being any the wiser. She certainly didn't want him involved in this private little war. Not only was he overly protective of her, but he was at the awkward stage of boy becoming man and would deem it necessary to show the Talliver boys a lesson. And she didn't want to jeopardize his relationship with Grady's sons. After all, like it or not, they *were* neighbors now.

"Mom, the tea's ready now," Eric called from just outside the bedroom.

"Be right out, sweetheart," Pamela answered, quickly getting a thick robe from the closet and slipping it on. She could take a bath later. Right now she didn't want Eric to suspect anything. Quickly towel-drying her hair, she put on some thickly furred mules, and as she strode from the bedroom, promised herself not to underestimate the little horrors again, nor to take country living for granted. After all, little varmints existed all over the country, and she would not be leaving windows unlocked from now on . . .

"Long time no see, stranger," Alice said the following morning when Pamela want to the hospital cafeteria for a cup of badly needed coffee.

Pamela slunk into her seat and Alice asked with concern, "Hey. What's wrong? You're supposed to look more rested, not less so, when you get away from this joint."

Pamela stole a piece of Alice's danish—she'd sworn to herself that she would cut down on unnecessary sugar, but she couldn't resist.

Alice pased the rest of it to her, and said, "Go ahead, kid." Her blue eyes shrewd, scanning Pamela in her forest green suit with rust and emerald blouse, Alice added, "Actually, despite those dark circles, you look a lot livelier than you did a couple of weeks ago." After sipping her cocoa, Alice set down her cup on the orange and yellow Formica table and asked, "Or could it be that you're looking so much livelier because of those dark circles."

"Why, whatever do you mean, Miss Alice?" Pamela asked in an exaggerated Scarlet O'Hara imitation.

"I mean, how is that hunk? The one you called me

so frantically about, asking what to do when a nurse—in this case, a stand-in nurse—begins to become involved with a patient?"

"I knew I shouldn't have called you, Alice," Pamela said, annoyed at her friend's astuteness. She had thought about Grady—and his kids—most of the night. And no clear answers were available. For while Grady's lovemaking had proved he *was* interested in more than her land, his sons' behavior showed her only too graphically how opposed *they* were to their father's non-business interest.

"Aha! So you're not denying it."

"Alice! Would you keep it down? You're informing the whole hospital cafeteria."

Alice looked about the bright, vividly colored room, which had plenty of natural light, with large windows and French doors leading out to a well-tended garden. "That's just your conscience speaking, kid," she told Pamela. "No one's looking nor hearing. But don't forget, I know you well. I can assure you making love with a man—and I mean really making love, none of those one-nighters that only serve to clear the guys' acne—does leave an indelible brand on a woman."

Pamela could not help laughing. "You are incorrigible, Alice."

"That's what the orphanage director said," Alice replied flippantly, then retreated.

Pamela looked at her sharply, but Alice had already hidden behind her wisecracking, impenetrable mask. Pamela knew her friend had not had an easy life—she had gleaned that much from Alice's meager, isolated comments about her life before Northern General. Alice was not a whiner, and accepted her vicissitudes in life without a whimper, picking herself up and going on. But she kept her cards very close to her chest, and though Pamela knew that there was some sort of painful mystery in Alice's past, Alice was reticent about it and Pamela respected her privacy.

"Well, tell Aunt Alice," she went on now. "What did this bad man do, besides love the living daylights out of you?"

Pamela toyed with her bent spoon. "What makes you think he did anything?" she answered evasively.

"Oh, come on. This is Aunt Al, remember? The one who saw you bleeding tears on the anniversary of your divorce."

"Yes, well . . ." Pamela looked at her watch and said, "Heavens, it's that time already. I'd better get going . . ."

"You're not going anywhere," Alice said firmly, grabbing Pamela's wrist and pulling her down again. "Tell me what's wrong. You know you listen to me because I care for you, and because I'm always right."

As usual, Alice could get her laughing in no time. Pamela quickly recounted the events of the past few days, and by the time she finished, Alice had tears in her eyes.

"I'd love to have been there," she said. "It sounds like something straight out of the Marx Brothers."

"To you, maybe," Pamela said, still not fully able to laugh about it. "But you're not the one who had to clean up the mess afterward."

"Yes, well, I admit there was a calamity in this comedy of terrors." Alice rolled her eyes, and Pamela, knowing her friend, narrowed hers. In a sad tone, Alice said, "All those beautiful wurst going to waste."

Pamela threw a napkin at her, and told her, "I knew yours was cupboard love. Just because you can't cook . . ."

"Now you've really wounded me," Alice told her, throwing the napkin back. Setting her elbows on the table and her chin on her hands, she said seriously, "Why don't you admit what the *real* problem is?"

"Well, I told you he wants to build this soccer camp."

"So? You can't hate soccer that much?"

"I didn't use to," Pamela mumbled. "But he wants to use my land for the camp. Grady Talliver is part of BNT."

Alice nodded, straightening. "Well, I must say you've picked yourself a no-win situation this time. Unless . . ." She hesitated, then asked, "Unless you would consider selling . . ." At Pamela's look, she sighed. "I guess not."

"I'm not being stubborn or just plain difficult, Al."

"I know. You took a chance, came out here to put your memories behind. You divorced your husband, but you were still in love with him when you did. And you can't escape all the memories because of Eric."

Pamela stared thoughtfully at the few drops of coffee left in her cup. "I couldn't live with Trevor's infidelities. I'm a one-man woman and expect my husband to be a one-woman man. Trevor never was that, although he's certainly been trying hard to be a better father."

"And Grady? Do you think he's a one-woman man?"

Pamela revolved the dark liquid in the standard-issue cup, and said slowly, "Yes, I think he is. In fact, I know he is." She looked up and smiled brightly. "I guess those are the breaks. I want my dream; he wants his." Fighting the wobble that had crept into her voice, she looked at her watch again, and said, "Thanks, Al. You're a true friend. But I've got to run. Talk to you later; okay?"

Alice looked at her with affectionate concern, and appeared ready to say something. But then she merely patted Pamela's hand and replied, "Sure, kid. See you later."

The day, particularly the afternoon, had dragged. Normally, Pamela loved her work, and the hours seemed to whiz by, but today she found it difficult to concentrate and lacked her usual enthusiasm. She knew what was bothering her: Grady had not called.

Pamela reasoned that he might call her that evening, and felt an immediate lift to her spirits. She suddenly realized just how far Grady had invaded her defenses and emotions from the need she had of just hearing his voice. Another voice—a tiny, nagging one inside her—was telling her that maybe their lovemaking, though wonderful, had not been as meaningful to Grady as it had been to her. There was still the question of the land hanging over their heads . . .

But Pamela would not let that tiny voice take root. She believed in Grady's integrity. She needed to believe it.

She looked forward to seeing Eric when she got home that evening, but found a note from her son telling her he'd gone over to Gabriella's to play on Benji's computers and to try some of Adam's new programming casettes.

She took a shower and changed into shorts and a short-sleeved blouse, and after starting dinner decided to go for a short walk to the lake.

She needed to get out for a while, but she had another reason for the trip to the lake: J.L. was now recovered, and he deserved his freedom.

About ready to let him go at the edge of the lake she shared with Grady, Pamela felt it would be more fitting to release J.L. where she'd originally found him.

Running quickly into the house, she left a note for Eric in case he returned before she did, and then she drove to the spot where she'd first met Grady.

After his remarkable feat of survival against all odds the day the Tallivers arrived, Pamela had transferred him to a large cage which Eric had fashioned. As if sensing imminent liberty, J.L. was unusually subdued, but his heart was racing.

Pamela walked to the edge of the bluffs and set the cage down carefully. When she opened the makeshift door, J.L. at first looked uncertain, disoriented. Freedom was within his grasp, but he hesitated.

"I know just how you feel," Pamela said softly. "I felt this way the day of my divorce. I knew it was absolutely necessary, but it's easier to go on living with the familiar, with the life of habits—good or bad—we've made for ourselves, isn't it?" J.L. cocked his mottled head as if listening, and Pamela encouraged gently, "Go on with you. Get! You're going to enjoy it. You'll see your friends again and enjoy the feel of the air against your wings and the beauty of the blue skies . . ."

J.L. took a tentative step, and when he saw nothing was being done to detain him, he left the cage.

It took only another second for the wings, both now whole again, to spread in the archetypal gesture of flight and freedom. Then J.L. was off, a graceful object against the cloudy sky, and eventually he became a progressively smaller spot of gray, until he disappeared in the horizon.

Pamela didn't know how long she'd sat on the edge of the lake but soon she noticed darkness gathering. Not so much from the late hour, she suspected, as from the clouds that were creeping in and erasing the last of the azure streaks in the firmament.

She thought of Grady . . . and then she thought of how relatively easier J.L.'s life was than her own. It was difficult in terms of survival, but simple in terms of decision . . . of choices . . .

Grady was coming to mean a lot to her, but Pamela reminded herself that she had just settled into a new life. Her house and property represented freedom to her. She didn't think her involvement with Grady—even if they were to marry—would place that freedom in jeopardy.

But she was afraid that if she did indeed sell out, it would imperil Eric's and her own happiness. His incipient relationship with Grady might be compromised if later on—however much that relationship progressed—she were to resent having given up her dream.

She had already given up one dream: that of a happy marriage to the man she loved, in a trusting, warm atmosphere, with lots of cheerful, healthy, loved children who would grow and develop and establish happy homes of their own. This was an ideal Pamela had yearned to fulfill to compensate for the lack of emotional closeness and adhesiveness in her own family.

She was afraid to give up another dream.

And as she once more looked at the sky, where the angry clouds had obliterated all brightness, she was afraid that when the time for decision, for reckoning, came, unhappiness would ineluctably be a companion.

She had a feeling that whichever way she chose, she would lose. If she gave up the land and house for Grady's soccer camp, she might come to regret her decision and resent him for it. And if she didn't and endangered her relationship with Grady, she might lose Grady altogether.

Not that she could be sure Grady loved her. Not yet . . . After all, he hadn't even called.

As the sky ripped open and rain accompanied her dash to the car, Pamela shivered. This flood burst seemed to be an ominous adumbration of what was to come . . .

Chapter 12

THREE DAYS LATER, Pamela rang the bell, holding an umbrella over Eric and herself. It had been raining steadily for the past few days. She closed the large men's umbrella when the door to the Talliver residence opened.

Big gray eyes peeped up at her, and Pamela smiled. "How are you, Damien? May we come in?"

Damien nodded vigorously and led the way. "Aunt Gabriella is in the attic," he announced like a well-trained butler.

Before she could stop herself, Pamela ruffled his straight blond hair, and saw the look of distaste on Damien's face—the same look Eric used to get at that age when his mother had committed the unpardonable sin of treating him like the child he was.

Pamela and Eric dried their feet on the welcome mat in the foyer, and Pamela asked, "Gabriella is in the attic? On such a gloomy day?"

"We've been helping her clean. And she found some real neat things. She told me to tell you to come up and see."

Pamela looked at Damien and felt an instant of uneasiness. Gabriella had said dinner would be ready at six, but to come earlier for cocktails. However, Pamela had run into some extra work at the hospital, and consequently she and Eric were late. It was already after six.

"Okay, Eric. Let's go see what Gabriella wants."

"No!" Damien exclaimed. "That is, Benji is waiting for Eric. He can come with me. We're going to play Pitfall and Galaxian and Pole Position."

Her suspicions once more aroused, Pamela looked into Damien's eyes and saw only innocence and serenity there. And after all, hadn't Grady said that the real dangerous ones were Adam and Craig? She'd already had that amply demonstrated the night of the party, with a double whammy: the suspended bucket of water and Craig's little souvenir, performed in record speed in the accommodating illumination of floodlights.

Luckily, she had not gotten a cold from the arctic, sudden shower. As for the big sign painted on the side of her house in huge letters: STAY AWAY. YOU'RE NOT WANTED, with artistic little skulls and daggers in the o's and a's . . . well, that had been water-soluble, dissolving in the first heavy rain.

But even though more surprises might lie ahead, Pamela had to face them. Smiling, she told Eric, "Have fun, sweetheart."

To Damien, she said with an assumed casualness, "Lead on, Macduff."

Damien took her to the back of the house, where a steep, tortuous staircase led—seemingly straight up—to the higher floors.

"If you follow this stair, you can't miss," he said, skedaddling.

As she looked at the dim-lighted, decaying steps,

Pamela had second thoughts. But she couldn't very well turn tail and run. She'd committed herself. If the boys had planned a little something for her, she had to go meet it. Even if it consisted of a welcoming committee of creeping crawlies.

Taking the folds of her dirndl skirt—as well as her courage—in her hand, Pamela began ascending.

Halfway up, where the crumbling steps met a musty landing, she heard a rustling sound . . . and turned to meet a skeleton coming out of the dark straight at her!

Having studied biology and handled skeletons in her anatomy classes, Pamela was not too impressed beyond the element of surprise. She shoved Mr. Bones away from her and saw it collapse at her feet as it derailed from the rail it had been ingeniously suspended on.

She continued climbing and suddenly felt something soft and furry crawling on her feet. While Pamela had never been one to scream at the sight of a mouse—particularly a wind-up toy mouse—she wasn't overly fond of the little creatures, either. Kicking the little fur balls aside, she suppressed her incipient anger . . . and stepped onto something that seemed literally to burst beneath her feet.

Swallowing hard, she stepped to one side to allow some feeble light to reach the floor and saw that the sticky substance adhering to her beige summer sandals was nothing more horrendous than a soft tube of green toothpaste. The color did nothing for her footwear or stockings, but at least it was not one of the dozens of unimaginables Pamela had envisioned.

Onward and upward, Pamela continued, coming to the upper floor. She could see the even trickier, smaller steps leading to the trap door. Before opening it, Pamela gave herself another pep talk, and was at least prepared this time.

A flurry of big, fuzzy spiders descended upon her as soon as she pushed open the door. Luckily, spiders were not on her phobia list, and knowing they were fake did even more for Pamela's morale, boosting her flagging courage.

Full of confidence, and more amusement than anger now, Pamela heaved herself onto the dirty, rotted floor of the attic, and was met with what seemed miles of spider webs. Grabbing an old baseball which stood in the corner, she cleared the way before advancing, and heard the patter of little feet behind her. As well as the splatter of little wings above her.

About to investigate the origins of these charming noises in the Stygian darkness, Pamela heard the unmistakable noise of a door creaking open. Anyone whose son had dragged her to *The Curse of the Mummy's Tomb* and assorted other horror flicks innumerable times would have called this opening of the door superb.

As she stepped forward, Pamela knocked into something. A table. And a candle on the table. With matches.

How convenient ghosts were becoming lately.

She quickly lit the candle, and turned in time to see the chef d'oeuvre: a mummy coming out of an ancient, peeling closet.

The mummy seemed to be wearing high-heeled boots and padded shoulders. But no matter. It was the thought that counted. And quite a creditable imitation it was of that classic of all classics.

In the flickering candlelight, the mummy extended its rather puny arms, and Pamela threw open her own arms, yelling with all the bad dramatics that had gotten her booed out of her one and only play in high school.

"My darling Nefertiti, you've come back to me."

A giggle escaped the yards of yellowing cloth teetering toward her, and Pamela realized her faux pas.

"Ah, Ramses. You noticed my blooper. You know I was always bad at those Egyptian names." Stepping forward, Pamela said, "But no matter the handle, lover, just come to me."

As Pamela practically ran to embrace her "lover," the mummy began backing up, and wobbled dangerously before coming down hard on an angular treasure chest.

On cue, a ghostly sheet appeared above her head, and eerie music came out of one corner of the attic, while a strange odor issued from an opposite corner.

Pamela advanced with determination, and just as she was about to catch her reincarnated friend, her feet disappeared from under her. Pamela sprawled flat on her face, and the culprits ran for cover.

Standing up, Pamela brushed at her smarting knees, and then at her beige dress, which was no longer that clean, light color. As she tried to recover the candle that, miraculously, was still lit, Pamela felt something crawling over her hand.

Only this time she could feel its texture and even its breathing—high horrors! Pamela let out a small scream. Fortunately, though, it was lost with all the other music the boys had thoughtfully provided, as well as the sound of mechanized bats overheard.

Her anger rekindled, Pamela searched the room with her quickly faltering candle, and found what she was looking for: a large bag. She began to gather all the little mementos the boys had left her, and swiftly headed for the attic door.

Hearing a noise on the steps right outside, Pamela hurried with her candle and filled the bag. Wanting to leave the room as soon as possible, Pamela unwisely put feet first without checking—and found her feet would not budge. Or rather her sandals. Her anatomy was still in fairly good working order, if a little dented and frayed around the edges.

Attempting to move her feet once more, Pamela came to the inescapable conclusion: Crazy Glue.

With weary resignation, she took the sandals off. She was really looking forward to descending this unique staircase in stockinged feet.

This time watching very carefully for any other strange additions to the surface of the steps, Pamela made her descent with no further incident.

"Pamela, Pamela! Where are you?"

Gabriella's voice was coming from the kitchen.

Pamela looked around and, seeing no little demons about, hid the bag. She would take her booty back at an appropriate moment . . . When no curious eyes were watching.

"Where were—What on earth happened to you, Pamela?" Gabriella asked with mingled amusement and concern.

Pamela saw the boys miraculously appearing and noticed their neatly combed hair, wide eyes, and collective air of apprehension.

"I was just looking over some things in the attic. The boys told me you might be up there."

"In the attic? In this darkness? Goodness knows what lurks there." Gabriella made a moue of distaste, and added, "But I told the boys I was going to feed the dogs in the garage. Sometimes they get too generous in their distribution of—" Her explanation ended abruptly as her expression hardened and she turned to the boys. "What have you done to Mrs. Shaw?"

"Nothing," Craig answered, looking as if butter wouldn't melt in his mouth. "We just thought we'd let her look around."

"Where's Eric?" Gabriella asked, alarmed.

"Playing with Benji's computer."

"Well, you get him up here, and then I want a full explanation of what's happened, after Mrs. Shaw cleans up."

But Pamela put her hand on Gabriella's arm and said briskly, "I'm fine, Gabriella. Really. Besides, this is a little secret between the boys and myself." Turning to look at four sullen, desperately brave faces, she said, smiling, "Isn't it, boys?"

They didn't answer, just nodded unconvincingly, and Gabriella said, sounding unconvinced herself, "If you're sure . . ."

Pamela smiled cheerfully and said, "I'm positive."

Reluctantly, Gabriella dropped the subject and led her to the bathroom on the first floor. But when they were out of earshot, she asked again, "What happened, Pamela? What did those rascals do?"

Pamela began cleaning up and said, "Acted like normal, healthy boys."

At Gabriella's pained grimace, Pamela said, "Well, a little beyond normal. But even though I'm rather angry with them, at the same time I'm amused and impressed at their intelligence and sense of enterprise."

"I know from Grady that you have a high threshold of tolerance and compassion, Pamela," Gabriella said, "so if you're even the teeniest bit angry, it sounds like some discipline is in order. Laurel was a bit lax, because she was such a prankster herself. And Grady has been more than usually lenient because of their mother's death. But enough's enough. I'm safe because I'm a lowly aunt, and therefore not considered a menace . . ."

"Really, Gabriella. It's okay. I went up there with a sense of . . . anticipation. It was sort of a . . . challenge. I had to meet it. I want the boys' respect, too. And I won't get it—or their trust—if I squeal." Bending to apply hydrogen peroxide to her scraped knees, Pamela added with a saucy smile, "Besides, I've never considered myself a snitch."

Gabriella exhaled air forcefully and threw up her arms. "All right. I give up. Be close-mouthed. Take care of it yourself. But watch out for yourself."

"I will. Stop worrying. I can be a formidable adversary when I have to be."

As Gabriella led the way back to the dining room, she muttered under her breath, "Yeah, but there's four of them, and only one of you."

Pamela laughed and hugged Gabriella's waist. As they approached the dinner table, all five boys were already there—four looking apprehensive, one looking puzzled. Pamela thought to herself, smiling, that the only thing needed to add to the gloomy mood of the Talliver boys was Mozart's death march.

Just in case, before sitting down, Pamela checked out her chair. Empty. There were no crawlies there, or spindly objects like a seashell or pine cone.

Dinner was delicious and quite pleasant. The boys were on their best behavior, and although Eric had some questions about her still somewhat disheveled appearance, Pamela was able to satisfy him with a vague answer. Eric was having too much fun with the Tallivers to linger long on his mother's mode of dress. As long as she assured him she was okay, he was willing to let it go at that.

Pamela did not see the use of confiding to him what had happened—at least not for the moment. Maybe sometime in the future, when everyone would be able to laugh about the boys' wily, adroit antics. For now, mum was the word. She would deal with them on her own good time.

The rest of the week passed quickly, faster than Pamela had anticipated. She found herself missing Grady, but knew her heightened mood was due to his call on Sunday night. He'd apologized for not calling sooner, but had explained things had been too hectic back at BNT headquarters. He told her he'd be coming back the following day. And that they would talk then.

Pamela had been glad when he'd called. Glad and relieved. Grady had given her his business card with his Ohio residence number scribbled on the back—that had been another one of his loose ends, putting the house on the market, since he intended living in Michigan most of the time—but Pamela had not felt like calling him.

She was unsure of her footing in their relationship. And she'd been unsure of what to tell him had he asked her what her decision was.

She was looking forward to Grady's returning. To his company, wit, and humor. And to a repetition of their lovemaking—only in something a bit less dangerous and novel than the hammock. The next occasion they made love, Pamela hoped they would have more time for more extended afterplay.

It would require careful planning and a real sense of logistics. Five boys between them, the youngest only seven, demanded down-to-the-minute timing.

Gabriella had agreed to stay on only until Tuesday morning, as Grady could not get back until late on Monday, he'd said. Since the flight was of such short duration, Gabriella intended leaving right after fixing the boys' breakfast. She was happy to be returning to work, but Pamela knew how much Gabriella would miss her nephews.

As for her, Pamela knew she'd miss Gabriella as a neighbor. They'd known each other only a short time, but had grown close.

After fixing a long, cool drink, Pamela took a quick shower and changed into white shorts and a short halter top, tying below the bustline, with cap sleeves. She'd purchased it last week, along with a couple of sundresses, a new bathing suit, and sturdy slacks and boots, which she'd need when she went camping with Eric on one of her upcoming three-day weekends. Walking down to the lake, she tied the ends of the orange-and-white geometric top more securely. Spying the canoe, she decided to take it out herself. It really did look old, but Eric had already proved its unsinkability. Looking out at the lake, she saw it was a deep aquamarine, reflecting the pure blue of the sky and the swift passage of a few marshmallow clouds.

After much pushing, shoving, and some choice, uncharacteristic swearing, Pamela got the recalcitrant boat into the lake. Although it wasn't hot yet, beads of perspiration were lining her forehead from the exertion.

As she was about to get into the boat, a deep, husky voice asked behind her, "Mind if I come along?"

Unable to hide her pleasure at having him back, Pamela swirled about in the water. "Fine help you are," she teased, "arriving after I've already split a gasket getting this blasted canoe into the water. I could have used some muscle earlier."

"Ah, but I did get here a little earlier. However, since the view was so outstanding, I had to take it all in."

Pamela's eyes gleamed like silvered emeralds. "I don't suppose you're talking about the lake?" she asked with soft menace.

"Oh, yes, the lake too, of course. But the other view . . ." he said, looking at the long line of legs emphasized by the brief cut of the white shorts. He sighed and closed his eyes. "What splendor. Such curves and healthy muscles . . ."

He couldn't finish as a large portion of the lake showered him when Pamela expertly hit the water with a heavy paddle.

Grady beat a hasty retreat. "Hey, is this a way to treat a poor convalescent?"

"Poor?" Pamela laughed. "Déclassé maybe, but certainly not destitute or pitiable."

"Well, how about letting a déclassé man row the boat for you? You can use my muscle that way."

"But your leg," Pamela instinctively protested.

Her eyes went automatically to his left leg, and she saw the cast was off.

"But so quickly—what did the doctors say?"

"That both your swift intervention and Kowalski's expert care saved me some recuperating time. So, want to make use of my muscles or not?"

Pamela looked him up and down in much the same way he had done to her, and felt her respiration quicken at the healthy picture of male before her, long limbs bare, strong and muscular, his trim body covered by rust-colored shorts, and a cream knit shirt that emphasized the breadth of his powerful shoulders.

"I must say, I would like to make use of those muscles," she told him, letting her gaze travel back up from his sandaled feet and noticing that his chiseled cheeks were flushed beneath the tan. "But I wouldn't say those uses are restricted solely to the canoe."

"You really know how to make a man's blood pressure rise," Grady said huskily. "Is it that you feel safe in plain sight?"

"As I recall, we were in plain sight last time those muscles—ah, exerted themselves."

Grady fairly leaped into the water, and swinging her into his arms, set her in the canoe.

"God, it feels good to be whole again," he said as he paddled away from shore.

"You felt pretty good to me last time," Pamela teased.

"One more crack like that and we'll be doing water acrobatics," he threatened seductively.

"I think I'd like a more orthodox setting next time, if you don't mind," Pamela requested laughingly.

Grady's beautiful eyes turned serious, and he said softly, "I didn't go over to the house with the intention of seducing you, Pamela. I did intend, quite honorably, to talk. But I got carried away . . ."

"You didn't exactly seduce me. I was quite wiling. And cooperative, as I remember."

"And exquisite, and soft, and silky, and as fragrant as a violet . . ."

"Could you please keep your mind on the paddling? We're going in circles."

"Sorry. I'm not the best of sailors—not when I'm presented with such a mind-bending distraction."

"Is that all I am to you, then . . . a distraction?"

Grady stopped rowing and met her gaze in a charged,

suspended moment in time. "So distracting I finished my business in record time, and delegated everything I could. I just hope everything doesn't collapse about me back at the office."

"I've always said that ambition tempered with a little lust is the best kind."

Grady let the canoe drift gently in the shimmering water and leaned forward. "There's more than that involved. I think I'm falling in love with you, Pamela."

Pamela closed her eyes at the husky declaration. It was what she'd wanted. It was what she'd feared.

When Grady bracketed her face with large, warm hands, she didn't draw back. While confusion and longing ruled her mind, passionate need ruled her body. His lips touched hers, cool and firm, and she felt the spinning of the boat transferred to her mind, her body swirling and swaying to the delicate, sweet caress.

She opened her eyes when Grady pulled back slowly, and seeing the question in his eyes, she spoke hastily, trying to postpone their discussion, wanting only to prolong the exquisite moment of communion. "I'm glad you're back to normal. And I know your boys will be glad to have you back."

"I already stopped at the house and changed. Gabriella told me the boys gave you some welcome the other night. But she said you didn't provide any details."

"Oh, the boys were just bored. They just got into some creative teasing."

"I bet. Pamela, you haven't answered me. How do you feel about—"

"Grady, sometimes love is not enough," Pamela told him quickly, and saw both satisfaction and wariness in his features. Unwittingly, she'd given him his answer. Sighing, she leaned back in the canoe, raising her face to the sun.

"You know, I was crazy about my ex-husband. I've always wanted a big, happy family. I tried as well as I could to keep it all together, but I found I couldn't tolerate his disappearing acts, not even to keep my marriage intact. Because it no longer was. Trevor expected me to lavish all my love on him, and short-change Eric. He was like a child, not wanting to give me all of himself, but expecting everything back."

Grady ran warm, whisper-soft fingers down her arm and asked, "You don't believe I'd be unfaithful, do you?"

Pamela looked at him and said thoughtfully, "I never really thought Trevor would be, either. And he wasn't at the beginning of our marriage. I guess the novelty provided its own strong aphrodisiac." She shook her head as memories, both bitter and sweet, played on the windows of her mind. "It wasn't jealousy that made me divorce him."

Grady lowered his hand and laced his fingers with hers. Pamela smiled at him and continued, "I just wanted a man to love, a man who would love me and my children back, just as I loved him, above all else. A man I could trust, whose priorities would match mine. Often, a person is lonelier and more unhappy in an oppressive, deceitful marriage than alone." Squeezing Grady's hand in silent gratitude for his support, she added, "Now Eric is happier, more ebullient. And Trevor is also happier, knowing he's no longer making me unhappy by betraying the vows he made. I know he loved me, as I loved him. But sometimes love is not enough."

"I think sometimes love is all there is," Grady told her, caressing the sensitive skin of her palm. "But how do you feel now? Are you content? Are you still in love with Trevor?"

She looked at him with newfound serenity. "No, I'm no longer in love with Trevor. I'll always have some affection for him, as my first love and the father of my child. But I'm satisfied on my own, doing work I love. Once I faced that big bad world out there, I found I could cope."

"You're sure you're over Trevor?"

"I wouldn't have made love the way I did if I weren't," Pamela said softly.

The canoe drifted languidly in the water, caught by a lazy eddy, the brisk breeze playing with Pamela's hair, holding it out for inspection by the sun, which gilded it in gold, then releasing it again to rest on her pleasure-flushed cheeks. "I gave Trevor another chance. But his infidelities became a corrosive at the fabric of my trust, of our marriage, and when they affected Eric so adversely, there was no other choice." Letting one hand drop into the water, Pamela sighed as the cool liquid stroked her inner wrist, and said with placid contentment, "I love my life here now. And I think I could stay on this lake forever."

"Present company included?"

"Present company *definitely* included."

"Well, I hate to break this to you, but you'd better go in. Your nose is starting to turn lobster-red."

"Spoil sport," Pamela said, and laughing, splashed him vigorously.

Grady retaliated—after extracting a very willing kiss in vengeance—and they returned to shore in a flurry of crystalline, cold showers.

As they walked into the house, the phone rang.

"Hi, Pamela," Gabriella said, her low, husky voice instantly recognizable. "I've been trying for ages. Grady said he'd go over to get you for dinner."

"Dinner?" Pamela asked, still a bit fuzzy from the sun and the excitement of Grady's presence.

"Yes, dinner. You know, the third meal of the day? Or did he forget to mention it?"

"Well, as a matter of fact..."

"Things must be getting awful serious if my dear lug of a brother forgets about food. But I imagine you two had something else on your minds?"

Pamela remained prudently silent, and Gabriella added, with mock offense, "Okay, be that way. Tell you what. I'll feed the kids and make you a cold dinner—salad, soup, shrimp. Okay by you?"

"Wonderful!" Pamela said enthusiastically.

"Oh, and try to remember to get here before midnight, okay?"

Pamela assured her they would be, and went in search of Grady. She found him in the bar downstairs, making a Bacardi for her. "I remembered," he told her, holding the berry-colored drink in his hand. She had asked for one at his birthday party.

"Did you forget something, Grady?"

"Forget?"

"Yes. Dinner? Your sister just called."

"Damn!"

"You're mad at your sister? Or have you developed a sudden aversion to dinner?"

"That's right. Laugh. The first time I see you in days and we're supposed to do something as prosaic as eat."

"We don't have to be there right away," Pamela told him throatily. "Your sister is going to prepare a cold dinner for us."

Grady's gaze glittered, and he came around the bar . . .

Chapter 13

"WANT TO FOOL around, Mrs. Shaw?"

Pamela slipped her hands about his neck and whispered, "Need you ask, Mr. Talliver?"

Grady placed his hands on her waist and with one quick, effortless movement, lifted her onto a tall, leather barstool.

He kissed the velvet skin beneath her earlobe, and tiny shivers skipped their way to her extremities. "Just checking," he told her as he left her for a moment and went to turn on the electric fireplace.

As he came back to her and put his hands on her waist, Pamela asked, "What about the bed?"

"Let's not waste any time looking for a proper place." His hands left her waist to travel to the undercurve of her breasts. "My thoughts have little to do with propriety at the moment."

As his thumbs glided over her nipples and her toes curled, Pamela murmured, "How encouraging." She hadn't worn a bra under her halter, and the heavenly friction was taking her to heated heights.

"Any objections?" he asked.

She opened her mouth to speak, but one of his hands lowered to her thigh, and started to magically knead the muscles there. Licking suddenly dry lips, Pamela said, "Actually, I can't think of a sound one."

His other hand abruptly left the swollen, aching mound it had been cupping, and lowered to her knee. With one bold, swift movement, he drew her knees apart.

A gasp escaped her parted lips and she remained immobile, feeling vulnerable yet excited, hot and cold at the same time.

"This—this is slightly unorthodox," she managed, the words emerging raspy and out of a constricted throat.

He pushed her legs even farther apart, moving in between them so that their torsos touched and her knees hugged his hips.

Their drinks were forgotten as Grady's hands went to her blouse and quickly opened the bow at her midriff. The one at her neck was next, and her top slid down her back, tickling the exposed skin on its shimmering descent.

Grady was already starting on the side zipper of her shorts, and Pamela watched with fascinated, fevered eyes before she brought herself out of her febrile trance to say shakily, "Grady, what if they come over here . . ."

"They won't," he told her reassuringly. "And even on the remote chance they do, they would make more noise than the U.S. Cavalry as they tramped from room to room. By the time they came down the stairs, we'd be decent."

Pamela's hands were unconsciously caressing the golden hairs on Grady's sinewy wrists, which she'd grabbed to stop his devastating advance on her clothes and libido.

"For what you have in mind, a herd of wild rhinos could be missed at the crucial moment."

He pressed closer to her in bold invitation and told her hoarsely, "We only have the fireplace on down here. Before they'd come down, they'd turn on the lights at the top of the stairs and crucial moment or not, we'd be aware of the blinding ceiling lights."

Pamela's hands lost their dubious authority on his wrists. It would be nice to relinquish control . . . Nice? It would be ecstasy to let go of herself in Grady's arms.

"I guess you've convinced me," she whispered, her hands going to his shirt and pulling it over his head. She wanted to see all of him.

Grady took one of her hands and put it on the swell of his manhood. "God, I've been going crazy with wanting to touch you and smell you and see you this past week."

Pamela lowered her head and pressed her lips to his shoulder. She felt him shiver at her hot touch and her hand caressed and fondled him through the tight confines of his shorts.

Grady moved back a fraction and pulled down both her shorts and panties with one fierce tug. Then his hands moved to her stomach, invading her navel with knowing, evocative strokes, and then lowering to the brown silk covering her femininity.

Kneeling before her, Grady buried his head in her lap and slowly, inexorably, pushed her thighs apart, allowing him access to her warm honey. Pamela bit her lip to keep the cry rising to her lips stillborn, but when Grady's tongue thrust inside and compellingly echoed the rhythms of love, Pamela could no longer hold her moans of arousal back.

Grady's mouth, lips, and teeth orchestrated a turbulent

attack on her senses. Pamela's legs, enclosing Grady's head, began to tremble violently, and her own head thrashed from side to side in a frenzy of need.

But before Pamela could reach the summit of release, Grady lifted his head from her throbbing center and kissed his way up her quivering stomach and to her nipples, where he deposited swift, shiver-inducing nibbles, before covering her mouth with his own.

Her hands caressed his back and shoulders, and when he took his mouth from hers, she lowered them to his tight, straining buttocks.

Grady moved closer, his hips positioning in the arch of love. But Pamela stopped him. "Let me," she whispered, taking him in her hands and watching him surge to pulsating life in her fingers. She stroked and rubbed, pulling and scratching softly, and Grady groaned, seizing her wrists.

But Pamela shook her head and sought his mouth, and Grady abandoned her hands and all protest and cupped her breasts, rolling and pinching her nipples as they each reached sensual furor.

Then he moved back to look into her eyes, and Pamela lost herself in the woodsmoke depths. Grady told her, "I love you," before his head descended once more toward hers, blocking out the flickering flames in back of him, and as he touched his lips to hers in a tender gesture of intimacy, Pamela felt tears well in her eyes. Meeting her eyes once more in the room's delicious dimness, Grady lifted her legs as he pushed forward to meet her and make them one.

His eyes held hers as he thrust powerfully, to the honeyed, readied depths of her, and Pamela gasped at the binding penetration. She could feel them becoming a single, wavering entity, and the blood thrummed thunderously in her ears.

The force and emotional power of the moment made

her eyelids start to droop, but Grady murmured, "Look at me," and Pamela fought to keep her eyes open in the fury of the maelstrom buffeting her to a swirling abyss.

Her knees tightened about him as her body became rigid and the first of the convulsions gripped her. Grady cradled her head and pushed her aching breasts against his chest, his eyes boring into hers as the storm overtook her.

Pamela cried out, once, twice, and still Grady held her, his hips moving vigorously, extracting everything she had to give. And when she began to ascend from the subterranean depths, Grady once more forced her into an eddy of blind passion, his strokes sure and potent, her name his cry of passion at the moment of violent release . . .

They dressed languidly, amid avid caresses and kisses, and as they left the house, Pamela picked up a gaily wrapped present from the table in the foyer.

"Another present?" Grady asked with raised eyebrows, but Pamela could tell he was moved.

"Couldn't resist it. It just seemed so appropriate."

Grady opened it and began chuckling gritty sounds that raised her hormonal level.

He took the T-shirt out of the plastic bag and spread it out. The shirt had the words DAMN SEAGULLS! printed on it in bold block letters, and on the shoulders and part of the chest, unmistakable splatters adorned the black cloth.

"That's about my exact sentiment," he said. "The artist could not have expressed it better."

"Well, they say one picture is worth a thousand—"

"Kisses. Come here," he told her, not leaving her much choice as he captured her waist and pulled her near.

Pamela stood on tiptoe and laced her arms about his neck. "Happy birthday."

"Lady, you're fantastic," Grady murmured, palpably hardening against her.

"Grady, Gabriella is waiting for us," Pamela reminded him softly as he began to get enthusiastic in his kissing.

Grady sighed and said, "Okay. Okay. Whoever invented relatives had a sadistic streak."

Pamela laughed, and as they walked outside, Grady said, "Thanks for the other presents. I may not have been properly expressive the night of my birthday but..."

"You had other things on your mind."

"With you around, I've got only one thing on my mind," he told her as he opened the car door for her.

As he slid into the driver's seat, Pamela said, "I thought all men shared that distracting flaw."

"Not all men share *you*. And it's you I have in mind constantly. Although I have to admit, sex isn't too far behind..."

She punched him playfully on the thigh, and Grady said as he started the car and headed back to his house, "Watch what you hit. I want to have another child some day."

Pamela stiffened, and Grady told her as they rounded the lake, "Pamela, I had wanted to wait, but I don't see the reason to. I love you."

"Grady don't," she told him, though her heart was fluttering wildly.

He parked the car in front of what Eric had nicknamed the Addams family mansion. She had no doubt of the depths of her love for Grady, but she was still torn as to what answer to give him.

"Pamela!"

But she escaped and ran into the house. The door had been left open and a loud recording of "Every Move You Make" blasted The Police sounds all the way to the dining room.

"There you are, Pamela," Gabriella said. "Brother following close behind, or did you two get into a fight?"

"Mind your own business, nosy little sister," Grady growled as he marched into the living room.

Gabriella shrugged her shoulders, unconcerned, and began clapping her hands. "Boys, your father's home. Come help me get dinner served for him and Pamela."

Dinner was a bona fide feast of cold ham, shrimp, assorted salads, and sundry desserts. The boys demolished their individual choices of desserts, which Gabriella had told them to wait on so they could share some part of the meal with their father. Grady did not eat as much as he usually did, and Gabriella's watchful eyes went back and forth between a scowling Grady and a distant Pamela.

"Hey, boys, how would you like a swim?" Gabriella asked, obviously aware of the charged atmosphere, and trying to give them some time alone.

"A swim?" The boys asked in unison, looking at their aunt as if she'd lost all her marbles.

"What's the matter, fellows? Afraid to go out at night?"

The boys looked at each other and Eric said, "That sounds cool to me. Mom never lets me go because I'm alone, but if an adult's there to supervise . . . ?"

Eric's statement ended in a question, and Pamela answered, "Sure, go ahead. But be careful and pay attention to Gabriella. She'll be in charge."

"Great!" Damien said, acquiring enthusiasm for the idea.

"What about the 'no swimming after eating' edict?" Adam asked. Pamela had noticed he was the quietest of the boys, but she suspected he was also the deadliest. Some of the stunts they had pulled the other night had to have been conceived and engineered by him.

"We'll play a game of catch outside. You boys need some exercise to get rid of some of that negative energy."

"That's a bunch of bulls—" At Grady's stern gaze,

Adam amended to, "baloney. And how are we going to play ball outside in the dark?"

"We'll turn on the outside lights," Gabriella suggested.

"Or we can use the glow-in-the-dark Frisbee," Benji suggested.

As the others quickly helped Gabriella clean the table, Adam got up and threw Pamela a blistering look out of smoldering green eyes that looked identical to Gabriella's, minus the warmth. Pamela recalled that the older Tallivers had had gray and green eyes, respectively, but she couldn't remember which had which.

Grady brought her out of her reverie and told her, "I know you want to avoid this discussion at all costs, but I don't want to wait any longer."

"You don't want? What about my wants?"

"Pamela, we're two adults. We should be able to discuss this sensibly."

"Sensibly meaning to your advantage. Listen, we're a bit addled. We've just made love and I don't think we've come down sufficiently from that high—"

"Dont' accuse me of thinking with my glands, please," Grady said, his voice low in his anger. "I've told you. I'm in love with you. It's more than sex with me."

Pamela got up and said, "Let's get these dishes done for Gabriella. She must have spent half the day cooking."

"My sister very diplomatically emptied the house for you. Please come upstairs with me."

Pamela hung back, and Grady released her arm with apparent annoyance. "Don't worry. I won't attempt to make love to you. I just want to show you some plans."

Reluctantly, Pamela followed him slowly up the stairs and into his room. She vaguely noticed that it was depressingly decorated, but it was big and roomy, and with larger windows it could be made into a nice master bedroom.

Grady went to the dresser, and Pamela saw he had a

model there: his version of the soccer camp, done in scale to its most exact dimension.

"I want to make the soccer field international size. In world class competition, that means one hundred nineteen meters—one hundred thirty yards—long by ninety-one meters—one hundred yards wide. I also want to construct dorms for the kids, offices and facilities for the teachers and coaches, and of course a gym, sauna, swimming pool, as well as recreational facilities. My property just isn't big enough. I need your acres, too—and then I'll have two adjacent properties, with the added attraction of the lake for swimming and boating and water-skiing in the summer. It's the perfect location, and it's the first one I've seen that boasts a somewhat isolated location plus the ideal terrain. I should know. I've been looking for seven years and only became aware of this locale when I happened to be here in Michigan on business."

"I see," Pamela said quietly. "And what would you do with the house on my property?"

"Tear it down, of course," Grady continued, enthusiasm infecting his voice and expression. "I want to have the best, most modern facilities, and make the most efficient use of the land. This has been a dream of mine for a long time, although I only began searching for the right area a few years ago. I plan to set up a fund for scholarships, so needy kids from the inner city who show promise and dedication can participate. I've seen some children as I've driven through slums who are geniuses with those balls—some of them ragged and beat-up, barely kickable. Yet these kids show the talent to be future Pelés . . ." Grady trailed off and asked, "Have you heard a word I said?"

Pamela had heard everything he'd said, but after he'd revealed his plans for her beloved house, the rest of what he'd explained had been momentarily lost in red-tinted film.

"Grady, if you want to have children play soccer, fine. Do it. But I don't intend to have my house demolished so soccer can be played. Let the children run around in your grass, your acres."

"Haven't you been listening, Pamela? I want to marry you. I want you to share everything—"

"Have *you* been listening to *me?*" She asked with the frustration that had been building since she'd pieced together his connection with BNT. "And haven't you got that turned around? Don't you mean you want to share in everything *I* have—be it ever so humble compared to your powerful, super-rich corporation?"

Grady paled, but his voice remained even. "I didn't realize you had any aversion to my wealth."

"I don't," she answered in a low tone. "Nor do I covet it." She shook her head as the confrontation she'd feared had finally taken place—and she could see no easy compromise. "I just wished you had taken care of the buying yourself. I realize you were trying to tie up all loose ends to be free to dedicate yourself to the camp, and that Gabriella was helping you attain your dream, but if you had come here sooner, personally, perhaps things might have been different." She continued and Grady left the table where he had the model of SETS—Soccer Emporium, Talliver Sports, Inc.—on display, and approached her as she paced furiously about the room.

When he tried to take her into his arms, she evaded him, and demanded, "Why does your dream have to succeed at the cost of mine?"

Grady began in a soft tone, his expression earnest, his gaze unyielding. "I told you. The children..."

"Are these children more important than us?" Pamela asked him as they squared off.

"You'd better calm down, Pamela. You're upset and frustrated, and not thinking straight."

"Oh, don't tell me to calm down. I'm perfectly calm! And seeing for the first time, really seeing, past the

Talliver charm and sex appeal. Why the sudden interest in marriage, Grady? Could it be that I'm not as malleable as you thought me? After all, a young woman divorced for a few years, she'd be an easy mark, wouldn't she? Most men I've met since my divorce seem to think so."

"I'm not most men."

"Don't take such a pride in that," Pamela told him fiercely. "And as I said, you'd better open your own eyes and look around. Your children don't want me. They've made that perfectly clear. And I haven't seen you do anything about it." At this point Pamela knew she was being unfair—she'd kept the details of the boys' dirty tricks from both Gabriella and Grady. But she'd gone too far to retreat, and she was too angry and hurt to think about fairness. "I've got to hand it to you, Grady. You're a real sharp businessman. Woo the lady, hit her when she's low. What was that lovemaking tonight for? To soften me up before you moved in for the kill? If I didn't know any better, I'd say Gabriella was in on it and you two had prepared the whole thing—"

"Say what you will about me, but leave my sister out of it," Grady cut in angrily. "She has nothing to do with this."

Pamela leaped on his words. "Then you're admitting there is a 'this'? You've only proposed marriage to get the property?"

Grady passed his hand wearily over his face. "No, I'm not admitting anything. There is nothing to confess to. Except my love for you." When Pamela remained silent and stared at him in seething frustration, he asked quietly, "Do you really believe that I would stoop that low, Pamela? Do you really think I would ask you to marry me simply to get a few lousy acres?"

"You thought enough of those lousy acres to invade my home and manipulate me into taking care of you," Pamela shot back. "And you've just admitted that this has been a long-time dream of yours—you've been searching for the ideal location for years. I imagine you've had quite an outlay of capital over this, made quite an investment."

"Yes, I've had a dream. And I still have it. But dreams are not mutually exclusive, Pamela. I want you in my life, too."

Pamela stared at Grady, knowing that this was the same man who had tenderly held her in his arms as she'd shaken in passion just a few short hours ago. The man who had invaded more than her house—her dreams and waking hours, as well.

But he knew what the house meant to her. And he'd declared his intention to decimate it with no thought of what it would do to her.

"I guess there's nothing more left to say," she told him, and slowly turned and left the room.

Chapter 14

"PAMELA! WHAT ARE you doing here still?"

Pamela halted and pivoted to face Royce Phelps, administration head of Northern General. He was a tall man, slender and full of vitality, which was needed to make the crucial decisions and solve the myriad problems inherent in the running of a hospital.

Right now, some of that vitality seemed to be lacking, his normally brisk step slower, and his normally crisp appearance less so.

"How was the conference?"

"The usual. Some new data—most of it the same old waste of time and energy. I just got in from Minneapolis. But what are *you* doing here?"

"Bill called in sick with the flu and Jenny's son has the measles, so I'll be staying tonight."

"But weren't you due for a three-day break?" As he

drew nearer, Pamela saw the fatigue etched into his thin, angular features.

"I was, but I can take it this weekend, or the one after next. We probably won't get too many X-ray cases during the graveyard shift—first of the week is not as bad as end of week."

Royce ran his hands through his umber hair and regarded her with a rueful blue gaze. "I guess you didn't think you'd be pulling double-duty when you accepted the position here, did you?"

"It's only happened twice, and I don't mind," Pamela said quickly, putting her hand on his white-jacketed arm. "I'm quite rested from that mini-vacation you approved a few weeks ago. And I appreciated your doing so on such short notice."

Royce smiled and patted her hand. "Thanks, Pamela. I'm glad you've taken care of one crisis. I'm going to check on a couple of things in my office, but I'll be at home all evening if you need me."

"I'm sure the situation won't arise," Pamela said. "You just go home and get some rest, and I'll—"

The electronic pager beeped, cutting her off and Pamela grinned. "Shouldn't have tempted the fates. Never say never in a hospital."

Royce gave her a tired smile and began striding away. "Maybe we can catch a cup of coffee later," he told her over his shoulder as he checked into the nurses' station.

"Pamela."

Pamela heard another masculine voice behind her, only this one had the power to warm her blood and increase her respiratory rate.

She turned and felt her heart quicken as it always did when Grady was near. It didn't matter that they had parted bitterly the night before. Nor that when he'd called her today, and he'd told her he'd hoped she had come to see things his way, she had not been able to agree. Her heart still swelled with love, a love she had tried hard not to acknowledge because she had felt their relationship doomed from the start.

As he neared, she noticed with surprise that Grady was wearing a thinly striped business suit and a white shirt on which a burgundy and gray silk tie contrasted elegantly.

His first words answered her unspoken question. "Something's come up and I have to fly back to Ohio tonight. Gabriella's already left and—"

"And you need someone to take care of the kids until you get back," Pamela finished.

"Adam assured me they'll be all right, but he's only twelve, though sometimes he acts as if he were older than the rock of ages. Anyway, cooking for four might be too much for him—at least, that's the official reason I gave him for getting what he calls a 'keeper.'" Pamela could tell he was nervous, unsure, because another of the reasons for their estrangement, which they'd discussed when he'd called, had been his sons' attitude toward her. He added uncertainly, "I could always take them with me . . ."

"Don't worry. They can stay at my place. I have to work all night, and I was going to ask Alice to stay with Eric. I'm sure she won't mind four extra boys. Alice loves kids."

"Alice?" Grady asked, obviously having remembered hearing the name but not quite placing it.

"Remember? Rank, name, and serial number only?"

Grady smiled, despite the tenseness evident in his expression and body. "She should be able to handle them with no problem."

"That's Alice. A regular problem-solver," Pamela said warmly.

A pregnant silence ensued. Finally, Grady said, "I have to go. Thank you for helping out, Pamela—"

"Don't mention it. Whatever may be between us, it doesn't affect the kids. I'll be glad to watch them for you for a few days."

Grady looked at her for an intense moment, then sighed. "I had hoped there wouldn't be anything between us—that you had come to see—"

"Your side of things?" Pamela asked wearily. But there was no rancor in her tone. Knowing Grady was leaving was making her feel empty, and she had no wish to fight when she could see how worried he was.

Despite the nurses' station a short distance away and the hospital personnel walking the halls, despite the unresolved differences and bitterness between them, Grady seized her waist and pulled her close.

Lowering his head, he kissed her good-bye: a short, hard kiss that tried to bridge what words hadn't. "Remember, I love you," he told her, and then turned and strode away, leaving the fragrance of pines and the taste of him behind.

"Well, how did it go?" Alice asked when Pamela got home the following morning. Alice had brought a change of clothes, and was already dressed in her nurse's uniform.

"Thanks, Alice," Pamela told her gratefully as Alice placed some scrambled eggs and a plate before her with a stern "Now eat it all and clean your plate."

Pamela didn't clean her plate, but did manage most of the egg and toast.

As Alice finished her cup of hot chocolate, she told Pamela, "You know, those boys were regular sweethearts. No problems whatsoever. Hard to believe an evil thought lurks behind those angelic faces."

Pamela laughed. "As a lady in the know said, you're no competition."

"You mean I'm not after Daddy."

Pamela raised her glass in a salute to Alice's way of

cutting to the heart of the matter. "For some reason, they think I am."

Alice quickly rinsed her cup and said, "I wonder what gave them that impression."

"Aren't you going to be late for work?" Pamela asked pointedly.

Alice glanced at her watch and said happily, "No. Got plenty of time. You can explain to me—"

At Pamela's pulverizing look, Alice left the room, telling her over her shoulder, "I put the kids in the basement. They all brought sleeping bags, and Eric joined them."

"Thanks for everything, Al," Pamela called out.

"See you," Alice responded, and seconds later Pamela heard the front door close.

Feeling weary from more than staying up all night, Pamela decided to go check on the boys, and then leave a message for Eric to give the boys cereal this morning, while she slept for a few hours. She would cook them a proper lunch, but she had to be fresh and alert for this evening should they need her again.

She saw the boys were still asleep in front of the fireplace downstairs. At least, they looked asleep, although Pamela thought she caught movement in one of the orange-red sleeping bags.

Figuring it might have been one of the boys tossing and turning in his sleep, she thought no more about it. Going upstairs to her bedroom, she began to undress and put on a housecoat. Debating whether to take a shower now or when she woke up, she found that despite her exhaustion, the thought of a cool, quick shower was irresistible.

Taking a night shirt out of the drawer, Pamela went into the bathroom. She yawned as she opened the door—and a full scream escaped her open mouth as she saw the army of lizards scurrying for cover within.

Wide awake now, she quickly closed the door before

any of the ugly creatures could escape—she thought she even saw a gila monster in there, although where in heaven the boys could have gotten one of those was a mystery. Putting on the discarded housecoat, she went in search of the boys. The hell with letting them sleep late. They were going to help her corral the uninvited guests.

She got a spoon and pan from the kitchen, and turning on all the overhead lights, clanged her way to the bottom of the stairs. It was certainly an effective wake-up device—and it didn't hurt to have noise precede her, in case there were any more nasty surprises awaiting her.

The boys were dancing around in their pajamas, some already standing up, others still fighting their sleeping bags. Eric came forward with a worried look on his face.

"Mom, what's wrong?"

"Those four angels, that's what." Pamela noticed that Benji and Damien looked quite convincingly mystified, while Craig and Adam had on tough, defiant masks.

"My bathroom's full of lizards. Anyone know how they got there?"

Little Damien started to look toward Adam's direction, then caught himself.

"Well, since no one knows, everyone will help gather them up. And how the heck did a Gila monster get to Michigan?"

"Oh, it's been de-poisoned," Damien explained, then realized what he'd admitted. He seemed to shrink under the withering glance his older brothers gave him.

"I'm glad of that, for your sakes. I'm certainly not touching that ugly orange and black monster. You're welcome to it. And I want my bathroom cleared out on the double. Understood?"

The boys nodded, and Pamela marched back up the stairs.

The undertaking took almost an hour, and Pamela had Eric help her search the rest of the house, despite Adam's assurance there were no more hidden live booby traps.

As she sat the boys down at the table and made sure they ate their cereal, she told them, "I want to thank you boys for having made my every moment so pleasant. There's nothing a person likes as much as to come home after having worked all day and night and find a bathroom full of lively, multicolored lizards. You must have gone to a lot of trouble to get such a variety."

Eric buried his head in his cup, a smile splitting his face. Pamela went on cheerfully, "It's also a nice way to repay someone who volunteers to help your dad out. I'm sure he would be proud of you."

As she replenished glasses of milk, she heard some very audible swallows. And Pamela was sure they were not attacks of conscience—at least not two of them, anyway.

Finally, Craig asked, "Are you—are you going to tell Dad?"

"And have him worried sick about you long-distance, when he can't do anything about it? He's got enough problems to cope with right now at work. Otherwise he wouldn't have left you so suddenly."

"It seems he's always leaving us," Damien said morosely. "And now that we've come out here, he'll probably leave us alone even more."

Adam dug his elbow painfully into Damien's side and Damien gasped, but he didn't say anything more. Not seeing why she should be defending Grady, but knowing that whatever his faults, Grady loved his kids, Pamela said, "Your father thought that this would be a good place for you boys to grow up in. All this fresh air, all this space. It's good for you and the dogs—your three P.I.'s will have all the room in the world to roam."

"So why are you defending Dad all of a sudden? You two had it out and I know Dad can't stand the sight of you. And I'm glad."

Pamela saw Eric's jaws stiffen at Craig's vindictive

words, but Pamela waved him down. She certainly didn't want to have the boys come to blows while in her care.

"There's an admirable trait—rejoicing over the misfortune of others," Pamela said calmly, and saw that the irony had not been lost on Craig. His gray eyes, so like Grady's, lowered, and he flushed violently.

"Well, boys, you get to clean up. I'm tired, and if you don't mind, I'll go to bed for a few hours. If you want to play, please do it outside, but no going into the lake unless I'm there." Looking at her son, she added seriously, "Eric, you see to it."

"Don't worry, Mom. Go get some rest. I'll look after things."

"Thanks, son." Turning to the four towheads, she saw two of the boys look at her with no appreciable antagonism, but Craig's gaze glittered strangely.

Uneasy, Pamela left the kitchen, but could think of no room they'd left untouched. Maybe Craig was just feeling resentful, and that was what his gaze had disclosed.

She stretched and without bothering to remove the housecoat, flopped onto the bed.

And was off like a shot, this time managing to restrain the yell that rose to her lips.

Why, those little—little—Pamela found she'd run out of adjectives strong enough for them. They'd bathed her bed in perfume! And not with an exquisite, expensive floral bouquet that would at least not offend the olfactory tract, no matter how strong.

No, the boys had bought the cheapest perfume possible. If they had even bought it—they might just have manufactured it themselves, Pamela thought, for she couldn't believe that . . . that odor was sold in stores—and by the gallon, it seemed.

She had noticed something when she'd come into the room earlier but had not come too near the bed, as the dresser was on the far side of the room. And having been too weary to pay much attention to externals, she'd overlooked this atrocity. No wonder Craig had looked so triumphant.

Pamela tore off the bedspread, which had contained the stench somewhat—and then the drenched sheets. The boys had obviously done it this morning. What enterprising fellows!

After taking the sheets off—she would have to wash all the bedclothes and air the mattress—Pamela put them in the bathroom. She'd deal with them later. Right now she was too tired to try to cope with dirty linen.

As she went toward her son's room and watched for any deadfalls along the way, Pamela resolved she would also deal with the boys later. And she knew how.

All it would require was Mother Nature and some creative shopping.

Chapter 15

"WELL, BOYS, HOW do you like the view?"

The four blond heads looked uninterestedly at the beautiful scenery, stepped cautiously closer to the edge of the precipice, and then looked back at her, eyes glazed.

"Ah, I knew you would appreciate all this beauty. I figured it would be worth it to drive north for an hour, to get us to this mighty fine terrain."

"The terrain sucks," she overheard from one of her disgusted hikers, but Pamela ignored the comment.

"Can we eat something now? We've been walking for six hours," Damien protested.

"Walking?" Craig spitted the word. "We've been *jogging* . . . jogging over this cursed countryside."

"Yeah, I haven't seen so many curves and ups and downs since I was last at an amusement park."

"There. You hit the nail on the head. That's what I'm

providing for you boys—amusement."

The boys looked at her suspiciously—Pamela had seen their uncertainty grow by leaps and bounds over the past couple of hours. She smiled brightly at them.

"Well, let's get going. We've miles to go before we sleep."

"Miles?" Adam asked, one of his rare forays into conversation. "We must have covered hundreds already. If we'd been heading west instead of north, we'd be at the Continental Divide by now."

"Surely you jest," Pamela told him. She had used the phrase quite a bit in the past few hours, ever since she'd seen the boys wince the first time she'd said it. The wince seemed to grow with every repetition.

Smiling, she led the way uphill once more, and a couple of hours later, called a halt.

"Okay. We can eat and drink something now. But make it snappy. I want to reach our destination and make camp before nightfall."

"Nightfall?" Benji repeated dully. "It feels like tomorrow already."

"More like next week," Damien mumbled.

As they ate some beef jerky and drank some water from the canteens, Pamela asked, "Where's your pioneer spirit? Don't tell me you're quitters. Because if you are, we can start back right now."

"We're not quitters," growled fiery Craig. "And besides, what makes you such an expert on everything?"

"I was a Boy Scout leader," Pamela replied, calmly chewing the dry food.

"Boy Scout leader!" Adam said. "How did you manage that? They're supposed to be men!"

"We had a shortage. Not too many men willing to take the job. I only did it for a year, you understand. But it's surprising how much one can learn in a year."

Craig got up, and said, "Let's get going. We've had enough of a rest."

Pamela hid a smile at his attempt at toughness, and at the answering groans that greeted his statement. Glad that hospital work and long walks about the country had kept her in shape, she got to her feet and said, "Okay. Let's clean this up. No polluters allowed on this hike."

Putting on the backpack again proved quite difficult this time, loaded down as Pamela was not only by the usual necessities inside her rolled-up sleeping bag, but also by little extras like a tape recorder, bottles, forks and other goodies. Plus some of the presents the boys had given her on that unforgettable sojourn into the attic.

Hiding her weariness and slightly sore muscles, she began striding briskly, and then looked back when the boys lagged behind.

"Come on boys! Let's move those feet! One, two, three . . ."

After another hour and a half of hiking over some rough terrain, Pamela finally announced, "Okay, this is it! We're camping here for the night."

Ignoring disgruntled comments, she had the boys put up their pup tents. After putting up her own, she went over to help little Damien, who was having some trouble with his. As her back winced in agony when she bent, Pamela wished she had brought Eric along. She could have used some help. But the whole purpose of this little expedition was for the boys and her to get to know each other better—and so she could teach them a salutary lesson long overdue. Eric had understood when Pamela had explained the situation to him, and had not minded staying with Alice.

Pamela knew that if she had told Grady about all the boys' stunts, he would have disciplined them. He certainly had no trouble handling them—although she knew he'd been somewhat more lenient because of the loss of their mother.

But if the boys were ever to respect her, Pamela, not just as Daddy's friend, she had to win that respect on her own. She was not about to run for cover, or to Grady for assistance.

For dinner that night, they had canned pork and beans, dried fruit, and some pop to drink. Pamela had instructed them to ration the water, and all but Damien had. She gave Damien some of hers, but told him that he would have to watch it from then on.

The boys were ready to hit the sack as soon as they'd eaten, but as it was only shortly after eight when they finished cleaning the campsite and made sure the garbage was all collected, Pamela wouldn't hear of bed.

"Come on! We have to have some marshmallows first, and tell some scary stories."

"I didn't bring any marshmallows," Damien said, regret heavy in his voice.

Pamela showed him the small pack she'd brought along, and told the boys to fashion pointed sticks for themselves.

As they scuttled to do her bidding, Pamela stretched, feeling each and every pain in her extremities and lumbar region. She'd ended up working two more nights, and Alice had covered for her, again finding no problem with the boys. On Thursday, Royce Phelps had told Pamela she had a three-day weekend coming, and not to come in until Monday.

So she'd taken the boys hiking—after making a hurried shopping expedition on Thursday after work—and now she was enjoying muscle spasms. It sure was wonderful to be alive!

When the boys returned, they began roasting the marshmallows, and Pamela began telling stories about wood nymphs, and then progressed to Sasquatch.

Pamela might not have been good at plays, but she'd always been a good storyteller. Within the hour, she had the boys watching the woods for any giant, lurking shapes.

Once she'd accomplished the first part of her plan, she suddenly clapped her hands, and the boys jumped half a mile. "Okay, boys, time for bed. Stay close to the campsite on nature calls."

She added more wood to the campfire, and built up a generous blaze. The clearing was quite large, and if any nocturnal animals got too curious, she could clearly see them in the intense light of the fire.

The boys got ready for bed in record time, and Pamela checked in on each of the boys to make sure all were properly covered. Adam very politely told her to mind her own business, that he was old enough to take care of himself; Pamela just as politely told him to mind his manners, or he'd be sleeping without a tent.

That shut up the one highly vocal dissident, and Pamela went to sit by the fire, draping a blanket about her, while she waited for the boys to fall asleep.

She had purposely put Benji's and Damien's tents closest to hers. They were not as vicious and intractable as their brothers, and she didn't want to scare them *too* much.

As she sat by the fire for over an hour, fighting drowsiness and muscle cramps, she also had to fight something else: memories of Grady. And having his sons around, with one having his eyes, the other his silky, corn-colored hair, yet another his mannerisms or way of walking, was not proving very conducive to forgetting.

Especially when she found she didn't want to forget. When she kept hoping that a solution could be found to their stalemate.

As her head drooped once more and Pamela found herself almost falling forward, she decided it was time. Quietly gathering all her implements, she began carrying out her campaign.

She began by laying some peculiar-smelling stuff in front of the pup tents. Then she wound some of the wind-up toys, and put them inside the tents. The boys were sleeping like logs and heard nothing. In Craig's and Adam's tents she also stuck some of those wonderful fuzzy, fat spiders. She put one on Craig's pillow.

Next were the sound effects. She had recorded a bear and a tiger from a tape she'd taken out of the library, and turned it on.

Still the boys did not stir.

Now for the finale.

She draped the blanket around her, grabbed some forks and sharp knifes, and approached Adam's and Craig's tents.

As she began her attack, alternately scratching and swatting the canvas between the tents of the two ringleaders, Pamela heard alarmed voices and a few off-color comments.

"What—what the hell's going on?"

"Adam, is that a bear?"

"Tigers, too?"

Pamela kept the scratching up only a second or two longer, then waited.

"My God, there are spiders in here."

"And rats! Yeeacchhh!" Pamela recognized Craig's voice.

"And what's that awful smell? Jesus, it's bear! Bears make that pukey stench. Holy Moses, look at the size of it!!!"

Pamela waited to see which boy got out of his sleeping bag first. Damien managed it, followed closely by Benji. They had obviously been somewhat frightened, although they were too sleepy to take all of it in. They immediately looked around for her.

But when they saw her between Craig's and Adam's tents, they ground to a halt. Pamela put her fingers to her lips, and the two boys tiptoed over, indicating to each other how Pamela, blanket-covered and silhouetted by the fire, created a huge, bearlike figure.

A few seconds later, Adam got out of his tent, saying, "Hey, these aren't real critters! And they look awful familiar . . ."

Craig also stumbled out of his tent, holding a large artificial spider. "What's the big idea? Who's the joker who tried to put one over on me?"

"Not tried," Benji said, laughing so hard he had to hold his stomach. "I'd say you were fooled, and real well, too. Tigers in Michigan!" He roared with laughter and choked out, "Huge bears!"

Craig was about to throw himself on his brother, but Pamela said, "Craig! Hold it!"

Craig stopped, and looked at her, startled. Pamela advanced on them, and said softly, "You don't seem to find this very funny. How come? Where's *your* sense of humor? Seems to me you can dish it out, but you can't take it." Turning to the oldest, she asked, "What about you, Adam? You're a real genius at scaring people. How come you're not cracking up now?"

Pamela knew she was pushing, but she wanted to appeal to their sense of fair play. Despite the perfume, the painted sign, the Gila monsters, the ice bucket, the unforgettable trip to the attic, she knew they hadn't meant to hurt her. They had just wanted to scare her off. They idolized their mother and were still trying to come to grips with their pain and anger at her loss. Damien, the youngest, had fared the best. But the oldest, Adam, and Craig, the one most like Laurel, had had a harder time.

As the boys avoided her gaze, she said quietly, "I hated having to scare you boys. But these stunts had to stop, and I didn't want to hurt your dad. Maybe I was a little selfish, too, because I wanted things to go well between us. You see, I think we could have had so much fun together if only you'd given me a chance. We still could." As four pairs of eyes converged on her, looking at her solemly, she added, blinking to keep the tears at bay. "Boys, I love your dad. But I would never attempt to destroy or erase your memories of your mother. I will never replace her in your hearts, nor would I want to.

She'll always be a part of all of you, and that's the way it should be."

Benji and Damien looked at each other, and Pamela could see that Damien was fighting tears. She opened her arms, and Damien ran to them. She embraced him tightly.

Benji also approached her, but since he was already a mighty ten, Pamela did not make the mistake of hugging him. She contented herself with ruffling his golden hair.

After a long silence, Adam finally spoke, lifting his gaze from a careful study of the ground. "I guess I have to hand it to you. You're almost as good as I am," he admitted grudgingly.

Pamela noted the "almost," but considered it a compliment of the highest order. And she would have accepted any criticism, as long as it was offered with an olive branch.

"Thank you, Adam. Coming from a master, that's indeed high praise."

Adam's blond head lifted sharply, and he looked at Pamela hard, but she could tell he saw nothing but sincerity there.

Fiery Craig shuffled his feet and exchanged looks with his older brother. Adam nodded his head imperceptibly, and Craig swallowed hard before speaking. "I—I—I'm—I'm sorry." The false starts, Pamela knew, were not due to any problem with stuttering, but with Craig's difficulty in apologizing to her. "I guess . . . we . . . I haven't been very fair."

"We're sorry, too," Benji added generously, and Pamela felt like kissing him. He was the one who had been the readiest to accept her, and he was such a lovable child, with a generosity of spirit remarkable in such a young person.

Damien nodded his head wordlessly within her tight embrace, and Pamela laughed, dispelling tension, as she realized she was impeding both Damien's speech and air supply.

"Sorry, Damien. I guess I got too carried away. Forgive me?"

Damien smiled and nodded his head happily, his eyes shining with remnants of tears.

Turning to the others, who were shifting uncomfortably, partly out of guilty consciences, partly out of the intensity of emotion, Pamela asked, "And will you forgive me, too? Adam, Craig, Benji?"

Benji said quickly, "Oh, sure. No problem. It was great fun. A real riot."

Pamela looked at her two rivals, and Adam spoke for both of them. "We had it coming," he admitted, holding her gaze.

Pamela heaved an inner, intense sigh of relief, and smiled at them.

"Well, what do you say we indulge in some more marshmallows before getting back to bed? The blaze is still big and high and I kind of feel like celebrating. Any objections?"

There weren't any.

On the return trip, the boys were subdued—except for Damien, who talked incessantly. Pamela suggested they stop at one of the crystal streams nearby and go body-rafting. The boys jumped at the chance, and the hours passed swiftly as they slid down the bumpy, rapids-like river.

After that they were all in very high spirits, and the rest of the hike was conducted quickly. As Pamela drove the last leg of the return trip, the boys fell asleep in the car, their cheeks flushed from exhaustion and sunburn.

Pamela allowed herself to hope. She knew all hostilities had not ceased, and that the boys would not become angels overnight. But if Grady and she were to have a chance at happiness—provided they could find an answer to their impasse—the boys had to learn to accept her.

And she believed they would in time. They were not truly vindictive. Of that she was sure. They had been well-loved, and showered with attention. Nothing would replace the loss of a beloved mother, but Pamela thought they were now really beginning to deal with the pain and putting the past behind them. At least the bitter parts. The memories of their mother would always warm them.

But if they would allow her, Pamela would like to take a new place in their hearts. She already held affection for them—because they were Grady's own, and because they were so bright, so alive, so . . . challenging.

She hoped they would give her that chance.

Grady returned Sunday, and he stopped by Pamela's to pick up his boys. Pamela noticed that Grady and Eric seemed to get along fine now, and wished that things would progress that quickly for her and Grady's boys.

As Eric, who had been helping her with the gardening, went inside to tell the boys their father had arrived, Pamela both dreaded and hoped that Grady would bring up the subject that was putting an invisible but very real barrier between them. But Grady only said, "I brought you a present. Do you think you could drop by after work tomorrow?"

Not knowing whether to be disappointed or relieved, Pamela said, "Unless I have to stay late. But you didn't need to get me—"

"Anything. I know. But I wanted to. It's long overdue—something I should have thought of weeks ago." Devouring her with gleaming eyes, he added, "And you can send Eric in the morning, if you like. I'll be home all day."

Pamela nodded, and was about to ask him to elaborate when the boys exploded out of the house.

"Hi, Dad," ever-talkative Damien said. "You know,

we had a great camping trip. Pamela really paid back Adam and Craig for all those stunts they pulled—"

Craig moved toward his younger brother, but Damien saw the move out of the corner of his eye and threw himself at his father, who picked him up and sat him on his shoulders. He patted Benji's and Craig's shoulders, while Adam held himself more aloof, contenting himself with an adult, if heartfelt, "Hi, Dad. Good to see you."

"What's this I hear? Craig, Adam?"

Pamela quickly intervened, "Oh, Damien was referring to the camping trip we went on, We sort of exchanged practical jokes." As Eric, who had been regaled with the happenings in great detail by Damien, coughed, Pamela fixed him with a severe gaze. "They're real troopers, your boys," she told Grady. "They tackled that hard terrain like pioneers." That much was true.

Grady's gaze sharpened, and he said wryly, "I can imagine. I'll have to hear their version of this interesting trip." Smiling at Pamela, he added, "You can give me yours tomorrow."

Pamela nodded, and Grady left with the boys. Feeling the emptiness that assailed her quite often lately, Pamela hugged herself and went into the house to get a sweater. She felt like going for a ride.

As she came to the spot where she'd first seen both J.L. and Grady, Pamela drove slowly and parked at the side of the narrow road.

She walked toward the bluffs, feeling a rising wind penetrate her thin sweater and tug at her hair. Sitting down on a rough, cold rock, Pamela looked into the distance, and watched the sea gulls that pirouetted in the sky.

She reflected on Grady's cryptic words, on her own feelings of late. She had wanted to teach the boys a lesson, but more than that, she realized now, she had wanted to remove all obstacles between Grady and her.

Only time could tell whether she'd succeeded with the boys, but Pamela realized that she could hold out no longer.

She loved Grady. As he had said, dreams were not mutually exclusive. She still loved her house and her property, but it would be *their* property. She hated the thought of having the house torn down, but she hated even more the thought of making Grady unhappy. And their being apart.

She'd always been looking for love, for affection. And trust. She believed she had found it with Grady.

She might have told him she suspected him of trying to get the house by winning her, but deep down inside she had never believed it. She'd said it in a moment of hurt, when she'd thought he didn't care for her, or not deeply enough.

But her house would be a cold and empty place without Grady. She believed she could have a happy life with him, raise a happy family. She wanted another child—she wanted Grady's child.

And no house could ever give her that. The house had been a symbol—it had represented her freedom, her independence, her own personal victory. But she had nothing left to prove. To herself or anyone.

When she went over to his place tomorrow, she would tell Grady that her house was his.

Early next morning, Pamela heard demolition sounds. The boys? No, it couldn't be. She quickly dismissed the thought. Even they could not make that loud a noise.

Dressing quickly, she got into the car and drove to Grady's place. A note from Eric had told her kiddingly that he was already at the Addams' mansion.

A small forest of trees hid the house from view at first, but when Pamela emerged onto a clearing, what she saw made her catch her breath.

Grady's house was being demolished. And the boys

were gleefully watching as the wrecker powerfully accomplished the job.

Pamela winced each time the ball hit the house, and she parked the car and ran to Grady's side.

"What are you doing?" she asked him, yelling to be heard over the uproar.

Grady embraced her and said, "My wedding present. I'll carry out my dream on a smaller scale." Releasing her, he took out a small package from his shirt pocket and gave it to her. "And here's another gift for you."

Pamela opened the box and saw a gold chain with a large, exquisitely carved charm in the shape of a sea gull in flight. She turned it around and read the inscription. It said: I LOVE YOU. GRADY. And the date she had run him over.

She raised tear-bright eyes to him, and said, "Why did you have to be so quick about things?"

Grady's expression underwent a swift change. In a strangled voice, he asked, "You don't want to marry me?"

Pamela laced her arms about his neck and kissed him thoroughly.

He was convinced.

"Then what are you talking about?"

"I'm talking about love. And trust. You should have waited. I came over here to tell you *I* was going to give you *my* house for a wedding present."

Grady's hug lifted her off her feet, and his kiss silenced her for a while. When she was allowed to touch the ground and speak, Pamela said, caressing Grady's cheek, "I once said love is sometimes not enough. But with you I've found what's essential to a marriage: love plus respect and a common purpose." Her eyes luminous with love and hope she told him, "I've found that essential triumvirate with you, Grady. I love you."

Grady hugged her again, and he ignored the whistles of the wrecking crew and the groans of the boys to kiss her once more. "I'm going to be establishing a branch out here. That way I'll only have to stop at the head office occasionally." Kissing her nose, he asked her, "Mind if I share your house?"

"Not at all. But we'll have to add some wings. The boys are growing quickly and will be wanting rooms of their own."

"Will do." As he wound his arm about her waist and looked at the five boys who were smilingly regarding them, Grady told her huskily, "I don't know what miracle you've pulled, but the boys like you. And you're right about additions to the house. We'll need them after we have some additions of our own."

"This feels nice," Grady murmured later that evening as Pamela snuggled closer to him, her hair spread out like a tawny cloud on his broad chest.

"Mmm," Pamela agreed, dropping a kiss onto the slightly moist flesh under her cheek. "I've missed the closeness and afterplay in bed. We've always been quite pressed for time. I'm looking forward to having a whole night with you."

Grady hugged her to him, burying his mouth in her freshly washed hair. The boys were watching a double feature in town—a suggestion they'd made themselves—and would be starting the second film around now.

"I'm afraid that with five boys, these moments are not going to be too easy to come by." He lifted his head to look into the hazel eyes brimming with love and passion. "Sorry you signed on?"

Pamela shook her head. "No, and I won't mind even after we have an addition or two."

"Ambitious lady, aren't you?"

"I'm marrying an ambitious man . . ."

"With lots of lust thrown in," Grady told her, grabbing

her by the waist and rolling her on top of him.

"The best kind, I've always said," Pamela smiled down at him as she met his lips halfway. Against his mouth, she whispered, "And such an inventive one, at that..."

Epilogue

IT WAS ON A late May day—crisp, sunny, perfect—the first anniversary of the date Pamela had run Grady over, that the fifth Talliver was born.

"How are you feeling, sweetheart?" a tired but beaming Grady asked his radiant wife.

"Just fine, Mr. Talliver. Are *you* feeling all right?"

"Never better. Bursting with pride and joy." While looking at her with such love and tenderness that he brought tears to Pamela's eyes, Grady took a small, square box out of his pocket. "A present for you—I'm glad our baby was punctual, although I could always have had the date recarved."

Pamela opened the box to a gold charm bracelet, on which a dainty, beautiful charm already hung: a sea gull with wings outstretched. The date of the birth and the correct name of the baby was carved in the back. The charm was identical to the one he had given her as a wedding present.

"But how did you—" Pamela began. Sitting up in bed, she asked indignantly, "Did you cheat and ask the doctor?"

Grady kissed her and laughed at her enraged expression. "No, I didn't. I wanted this baby to be a complete surprise to me, just like you did. And I can't say that I guessed right, either. I had a charm of each made—with a girl's and boy's name. I was fairly confident a Talliver would not let me down and not appear on the expected date."

Pamela smiled and threw her arms about her husband's neck. "You are sounding quite self-satisfied, Grady Talliver. I'lll have to fix that when I get out of this hospital tomorrow."

Grady shook his head. "A few more days, sweetheart. The doctor wants to make sure you're all right. After all, you did have a hard time giving birth to Eric."

"But many first births are difficult," Pamela began, ready to go home right now, and intending to tell her husband so. But at the worried look on Grady's face, she subsided and kissed him, saying, "I love you, Grady Talliver. And I'm so happy I could cry. I have my dream: a big, happy family."

"I think you are crying, sweetheart," Grady said, tears shining in his own eyes. "It's amazing how you didn't cry during labor, though." He dried the salty pearls with a loving mouth, and said, "God, how I love you, Pamela. When I realized how insensitive I'd been, talking so easily of destroying your home, I was afraid I'd lost you."

"Never," Pamela said fervently. "Despite all the obstacles—first my son, then yours, then the property, we're together. We've both fulfilled our dreams."

A nurse bustled in and clucked disapprovingly. "None of that, now. No hanky-panky. You have to give your wife a chance to rest before starting on the next one, Mr. Talliver."

The nurse deposited the precious, vociferous bundle at Pamela's breast and as the baby began to avidly search for its mother's milk, the nurse said, "Seems baby Talliver's starving."

"Runs in the family," Pamela said as the nurse fixed the pillow for her.

Pamela opened her maternity gown and pressed her breast against the baby's cheek, positioning the nipple. The tiny mouth began greedily sucking in air, and quickly honed in on its destination, while Pamela checked the perfect little body and Grady played with the baby's busy toes.

After the nurse had left, Grady sat down on the bed once more, ignoring the stern Northern General regulations, and said, "About starting that other baby . . ."

Pamela raised her eyebrows, and said, "And you told me *I* was ambitious."

Grady caressed his wife's pink cheek and the infant's ruddy one. "I guess I ought to warn you. Twins *do* run in the family . . ."

The newest Talliver captured the big masculine thumb held so temptingly within reach, and stopped its diverting tickling.

"Perfect!" Pamela exclaimed. "I had been a bit worried about not being able to continue the chain—Adam, Benji, Craig, Damien, Eric. But with twins, I have the perfect name to add to Helena."

"You're so sure about next time? Both twins and girls?"

"Positive," Pamela smiled at him.

"And what's the name?"

"Gabriella."

Grady's eyes gleamed as he looked at her over the bald top of the infant's head. Kissing the delicate crown very carefully, he told her, "The perfect solution. And let's hope we do get our girls."

As they both held hands over the baby's healthy, nine pound six ounce body, Pamela and Grady looked entranced as Ferguson Scott Talliver partook of his first meal in true Talliver fashion.

____0-425-07773-X **INTRUDER'S KISS #246** Carole Buck $2.25
____0-425-07774-8 **LADY BE GOOD #247** Elissa Curry $2.25
____0-425-07775-6 **A CLASH OF WILLS #248** Lauren Fox $2.25
____0-425-07776-4 **SWEPT AWAY #249** Jacqueline Topaz $2.25
____0-425-07975-9 **PAGAN HEART #250** Francine Rivers $2.25
____0-425-07976-7 **WORDS OF ENDEARMENT #251** Helen Carter $2.25
____0-425-07977-5 **BRIEF ENCOUNTER #252** Aimée Duvall $2.25
____0-425-07978-3 **FOREVER EDEN #253** Christa Merlin $2.25
____0-425-07979-1 **STARDUST MELODY #254** Mary Haskell $2.25
____0-425-07980-5 **HEAVEN TO KISS #255** Charlotte Hines $2.25
____0-425-08014-5 **AIN'T MISBEHAVING #256** Jeanne Grant $2.25
____0-425-08015-3 **PROMISE ME RAINBOWS #257** Joan Lancaster $2.25
____0-425-08016-1 **RITES OF PASSION #258** Jacqueline Topaz $2.25
____0-425-08017-X **ONE IN A MILLION #259** Lee Williams $2.25
____0-425-08018-8 **HEART OF GOLD #260** Liz Grady $2.25
____0-425-08019-6 **AT LONG LAST LOVE #261** Carole Buck $2.25
____0-425-08150-8 **EYE OF THE BEHOLDER #262** Kay Robbins $2.25
____0-425-08151-6 **GENTLEMAN AT HEART #263** Elissa Curry $2.25
____0-425-08152-4 **BY LOVE POSSESSED #264** Linda Barlow $2.25
____0-425-08153-2 **WILDFIRE #265** Kelly Adams $2.25
____0-425-08154-0 **PASSION'S DANCE #266** Lauren Fox $2.25
____0-425-08155-9 **VENETIAN SUNRISE #267** Kate Nevins $2.25
____0-425-08199-0 **THE STEELE TRAP #268** Betsy Osborne $2.25
____0-425-08200-8 **LOVE PLAY #269** Carole Buck $2.25
____0-425-08201-6 **CAN'T SAY NO #270** Jeanne Grant $2.25
____0-425-08202-4 **A LITTLE NIGHT MUSIC #271** Lee Williams $2.25
____0-425-08203-2 **A BIT OF DARING #272** Mary Haskell $2.25
____0-425-08204-0 **THIEF OF HEARTS #273** Jan Mathews $2.25
____0-425-08284-9 **MASTER TOUCH #274** Jasmine Craig $2.25
____0-425-08285-7 **NIGHT OF A THOUSAND STARS #275** Petra Diamond $2.25
____0-425-08286-5 **UNDERCOVER KISSES #276** Laine Allen $2.25
____0-425-08287-3 **MAN TROUBLE #277** Elizabeth Henry $2.25
____0-425-08288-1 **SUDDENLY THAT SUMMER #278** Jennifer Rose $2.25
____0-425-08289-X **SWEET ENCHANTMENT #279** Diana Mars $2.25

Prices may be slightly higher in Canada.

Available at your local bookstore or return this form to:

SECOND CHANCE AT LOVE
Book Mailing Service
P.O. Box 690, Rockville Centre, NY 11571

Please send me the titles checked above. I enclose ______ Include 75¢ for postage and handling if one book is ordered; 25¢ per book for two or more not to exceed $1.75. California, Illinois, New York and Tennessee residents please add sales tax.

NAME________________________________

ADDRESS______________________________

CITY____________________ STATE/ZIP____________

(allow six weeks for delivery) **SK-41b**

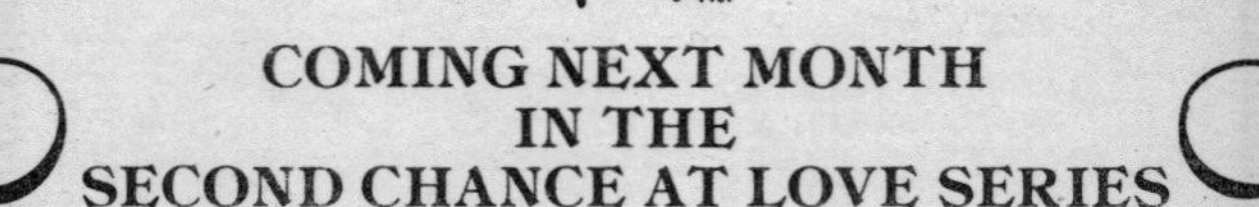

COMING NEXT MONTH IN THE SECOND CHANCE AT LOVE SERIES

SUCH ROUGH SPLENDOR #280 by Cinda Richards
When Amelia Taylor confronts Houston "Mac" McDade—the orneriest, gentlest, dumbest, smartest, most exasperating cow puncher alive—his unorthodox pursuit both alarms and arouses her, endangering her sanity...and her heart!

WINDFLAME #281 by Sarah Crewe
To college fundraiser Melissa Markham, wealth alumnus Dakin Quarry is big game. But the only "endowments" he's interested in are hers!

STORM AND STARLIGHT #282 by Lauren Fox
Larger than life Eric Nielson fills Maggie McGuire's life with zest and passion, but her company's policies are driving a wedge between them...and threatening Eric's satellite-dish manufacturing company.

HEART OF THE HUNTER #283 by Liz Grady
Bounty hunter Mitch Cutter's been hired to hunt down Leigh Bramwell, but her soft innocence and plucky defiance short-circuit his ruthless professionalism ...and make him ache to protect her.

LUCKY'S WOMAN #284 by Delaney Devers
Bedeviled by bayou alligators, a rangy rooster, and a raccoon named Alphonse, ladylike Summer strives to be "woman" enough for earthy, virile "Lucky" Verret—the husband she loved and lost.

PORTRAIT OF A LADY #285 by Elizabeth N. Kary
When Paige Fenton declares the painting a forgery, she comes up against its complex, unpredictable owner, Grant Hamilton, who obviously intends to buy her cooperation with kisses.

QUESTIONNAIRE

1. How do you rate ______________________________

(please print TITLE)

☐ excellent ☐ good

☐ very good ☐ fair ☐ poor

2. How likely are you to purchase another book in this series?

☐ definitely would purchase

☐ probably would purchase

☐ probably would not purchase

☐ definitely would not purchase

3. How likely are you to purchase another book by this author?

☐ definitely would purchase

☐ probably would purchase

☐ probably would not purchase

☐ definitely would not purchase

4. How does this book compare to books in other contemporary romance lines?

☐ much better

☐ better

☐ about the same

☐ not as good

☐ definitely not as good

5. Why did you buy this book? (Check as many as apply)

☐ I have read other SECOND CHANCE AT LOVE romances

☐ friend's recommendation

☐ bookseller's recommendation

☐ art on the front cover

☐ description of the plot on the back cover

☐ book review I read

☐ other ______________________________

____

____

(Continued...)

6. Please list your three favorite contemporary romance lines.

____

____

7. Please list your favorite authors of contemporary romance lines.

____

____

____

____

____

____

8. How many SECOND CHANCE AT LOVE romances have you read? ________________

9. How many series romances like SECOND CHANCE AT LOVE do you <u>read</u> each month? ________

10. How many series romances like SECOND CHANCE AT LOVE do you <u>buy</u> each month? ________

11. Mind telling your age?
    - ☐ under 18
    - ☐ 18 to 30
    - ☐ 31 to 45
    - ☐ over 45

☐ Please check if you'd like to receive our <u>free</u> SECOND CHANCE AT LOVE Newsletter.

We hope you'll share your other ideas about romances with us on an additional sheet and attach it securely to this questionnaire.

• •

Fill in your name and address below:

Name ____________________________

Street Address ________________________

City ____________ State ____________ Zip ________

Please return this questionnaire to:

SECOND CHANCE AT LOVE
The Berkley Publishing Group
200 Madison Avenue, New York, New York 10016